TER

GW00367394

Nurse Vonne Lothian was an identical
twin—something which she found was not
always an advantage. Especially when her
sister persuaded her to swop places on a
year's contract at a private hospital in the
Northern territory of Australia. For the
man her sister had jilted just happened to
be the visiting gynaecologist!

Judith Worthy lives in an outer suburb of Melbourne, Australia, with her husband. When not writing she can usually be found bird-watching or gardening. She also likes to listen to music, and the radio, paints a little, likes to travel and is concerned about conservation and animal cruelty. As well as romantic fiction, she also writes books for children.

TERRITORY NURSE

BY
JUDITH WORTHY

MILLS & BOON LIMITED
15–16 BROOK'S MEWS
LONDON W1A 1DR

CHAPTER ONE

THE lights in the jumbo jet's cabin were still dimmed when Vonne Lothian quietly raised the blind on her window and peered out into the vastness of space. At first there was only star-studded darkness, but, as her eyes adjusted, she glimpsed beyond the tip of the long grey wing a faint light streaking the sky along the rim of the earth.

Dawn—which meant she was nearing her destination, Darwin, in the Northern Territory of Australia.

Her stomach gave a nervous lurch and she moistened her lips, thinking for the millionth time since she had left London that she must be crazy to have let Vicky talk her into coming.

She stretched her legs wearily. She had not slept at all during the flight from Singapore. She was too keyed up. Even having three seats to herself and being able to lie out quite comfortably had not helped. She had tried to read a novel to pass the time, but nothing could distract her thoughts.

In Darwin she would have to face Kirk Leveson. For hours she had been trying to imagine his reaction to her news, which was made all the more impossible since she hardly knew him. She had only met him once, but she recalled his face remarkably clearly—pleasantly rugged features, deeply suntanned, deep-set hazel eyes with tiny laughter lines spraying out at their corners, a look of quizzical amusement, a wide firm mouth deeply indented at the corners when he smiled. Unruly dark blond hair.

He would not be smiling today, though. Not after he had heard her news. There would be no quizzical

5

amusement in his eyes.

I shouldn't have come, Vonne thought, panic tightening her chest muscles. Then she instantly contradicted herself. But how could I have let Vicky down—or the hospital . . . ?

With a deep sigh she tucked her long slender legs under her and leaned back against the much-pummelled airline pillow. She wished with all her heart that her twin sister had not inveigled her into this ghastly situation, which grew worse and worse in her imagination the closer she came to her destination.

'*Please*, Vonne . . .' Vicky had begged desperately when Vonne had at first flatly refused. '*Please* . . .' She had reinforced her plea with the reminder, 'You owe me a favour!'

Repayment was something Vicky would never have claimed in normal circumstances. The favours the sisters did for each other were freely bestowed with no strings attached.

The favour Vicky had referred to, however, had been a particularly generous one. Without her sister's help and insistence, Vonne would never have taken the much-needed month's holiday in the Caribbean, where she had tried heroically to pull herself together after the disaster of Leith.

Foolishly, she had fallen in love with a patient. She had nursed Leith Forbes for over a year, living in the same house as him and his mother, while she helped him to rehabilitate after a bad car accident. The knowledge that he might never walk again had not stopped her falling in love with him, as it had apparently caused his fiancée to fall out of love with him.

Vonne had found herself in the role of comforter as well as nurse, and as a consequence had been more vulnerable. It had been a joyous discovery when it seemed that the doctors might be wrong and Leith would walk again after all. He had declared that it would never have happened but for Vonne and her devotion.

But Vonne's joy had been short-lived. Leith's fiancée had suddenly reappeared, contrite, and eager to take up where they had left off. Discovering that Leith still loved Angela after all, and that what he had felt for *her* had been no more than gratitude and affection, had been a bitter blow to Vonne. Only Vicky understood the depth of her misery. Like most identical twins they were very close and they had always, since they were little girls, been intensely loyal to each other. There was nothing one would not do for the other.

Vicky had made it possible for Vonne to spend a month in Barbados instead of the brief holiday she could have afforded herself. Now Vonne was repaying that favour. Although she would have done it anyway, she thought ruefully.

Although they were identical in looks, both having short, curly auburn hair, dark brown velvety eyes fringed by long luxuriant lashes, softly curving (and what Leith had called in Vonne 'very kissable') lips, and slender but curvaceous figures, they were not entirely identical in temperament, on the surface at least.

Both were fiercely independent, having no close family since their parents had died when the twins were in their teens. Both had an adventurous streak, but Vonne tended to be more cautious than Vicky. Vicky was the eternal optimist and inclined to be reckless, Vonne, though impulsive too, was more often prey to misgivings. Both were warm and generous with affection, but Vonne was less flamboyant than her sister. Vicky wore her heart on her sleeve sometimes, Vonne never did. They were, as a friend of Vicky's had once remarked, like chocolates that looked the same but had different centres with different flavours!

'Vicky, are you really sure?' Anxiously Vonne had repeatedly asked the question after her twin had dropped her bombshell only three days before they were due to fly out together to Darwin. 'Are you sure this isn't just a temporary infatuation—I mean, it could be just a cover-up for last-minute nerves?'

Vicky, serious as a judge, raked her curls with agitated fingers and her mouth took on a stubborn set. 'No, Vonne, I'm quite sure. Getting engaged to Kirk was a mistake. He—he rushed me, because of his having to go back to Australia.' She laughed regretfully. 'Oh, Vonne, I don't know what made me think a life in the Australian outback, thousands of miles from England, was what I wanted. At first it seemed so romantic and I suppose I got carried away . . .'

'Aren't you getting a bit carried away with Armand too?' Vonne observed dryly. Vicky had known the handsome French doctor for only a few weeks.

Vicky's eyes were innocently wide. 'This is different, Vonne. I *know* Armand is Mr Right.'

'You still won't be living in England,' Vonne reminded her.

But Vicky was confident. 'Paris isn't far from London, love.'

Vonne was still doubtful. 'I really don't think I should go—not in the circumstances,' she protested.

Vicky, however, would not be dissuaded. 'Of course you must go. You've got a year's contract at the hospital and you'll be letting them down if you don't. You can't back out of that just because of me, Vonne.'

'But I wouldn't have been going in the first place if it hadn't been for you!' Vonne exclaimed, exasperated.

Vicky said gently, 'Vonne darling, it's what you need right now.' Her eyes softened with concern. She knew that Vonne's heart was still fragile.

While her sister was away in Barbados, Vicky had arranged a year's contract for Vonne at the private hospital in Darwin where the man she was to jilt was a visiting gynaecologist/obstetrician. Vicky had known that the West Indian interlude might not effect a total cure, and since Vonne had already agreed to fly out with her to be bridesmaid at the wedding, she had asked Kirk to organise it so that she could stay on for a while.

Vonne had readily agreed to the plan when Vicky had written to tell her about it. A complete change of environment might help her to forget Leith. But now Vicky was going to France instead, with Armand Saint-Germain, a charming French radiologist she had met in the rather exclusive clinic where she worked, and she wanted Vonne to go to Australia as planned and break the dreadful news to Kirk that she could not marry him after all.

'It'll be kinder if you tell him personally,' Vicky explained. 'I'm hopeless at expressing myself in a letter and it would be even more difficult on the phone. I'll write a letter, of course, for you to take with you, but I know you'll explain it so he understands. I don't want him to be hurt, Vonne . . .'

'But he will be hurt!' Vonne had expostulated, coming as close to anger with her twin as she had ever been. 'He loves you!'

'I know—I know . . .' Vicky wailed in anguish. 'It's not that I'm unfeeling, Vonne, it's just that—I can't *help* it, I *love* Armand!' Tears glistened in her eyes and she wrung her slender hands. '*Please*, Vonne—do this for me and I'll never ask you to do me another favour.'

Vicky was so distressed that Vonne felt her opposition melting in spite of her better judgment. Reluctantly she allowed herself to be persuaded. With a sinking heart and grave misgivings about the wisdom of it, she had left London as planned, but without the bridesmaid's dress she had bought for Vicky's wedding.

Vonne glanced out of the plane window again. The sky was lightening rapidly and there was a tinge of pink on the eastern horizon. Below lay the dark Timor Sea. She glanced at her watch. Any minute now there would be an announcement. People were stirring in their seats, flight attendants were moving about. The plane was in fact three hours late, having been delayed on the ground at Singapore, which meant that instead of arriving around four a.m. they would be landing nearer to breakfast-time.

A flight attendant offered Vonne a glass of orange juice. Feeling decidedly scruffy herself, Vonne wondered how the girl managed to keep such a chic, well-groomed appearance on long flights. The only consolation was that she would have been feeling a lot worse if she hadn't had a day's stopover in Singapore.

She accepted a glass from the tray, and as she did so the captain announced their imminent arrival in Darwin and gave local time and weather conditions. Vonne only half took it in.

Suddenly she was remembering vividly the one and only time she had met Kirk Leveson. It had left an indelible imprint on her mind, for a very good reason. Even now she could not recall it without a hot flush of embarrassment.

It had been at his and Vicky's engagement party in London, a few months ago. Her relationship with Leith had been blossoming then and she had been happily anticipating just such a party for herself in the near future—if perhaps a rather more subdued one.

On that unusually mild early spring evening she had been standing on the terrace of Vicky's Australian friend Sylvia's house in Hampstead where the party was being held, musing romantically on the future that had then seemed so promising. She had just been talking to Vicky about it. They had not seen much of each other since Vonne had gone down to Cornwall to nurse Leith, so both had a lot of news to exchange. It was wonderful, Vicky had said, that they had both fallen in love at the same time. Then, anxious because Kirk was late, she had hurried back inside in case he had arrived.

'I'm dying for you to meet him,' she enthused,

starry-eyed and bubbling over with excitement. 'He's absolutely gorgeous!'

Vonne had met him only a few minutes later, but in circumstances she shuddered to recall. A man came out of the house saying, 'Ah—there you are! Sylvia said you were out here.'

At the sound of the deep masculine voice with an Australian accent, Vonne turned from looking pensively down the garden, not realising at first who he was. Sylvia had a lot of Australian friends and it was through her that Vicky had met Kirk.

Her face must have registered her puzzlement that he knew her when she didn't recognise him, but he didn't seem to notice. He walked up to her and his arms encircled her possessively. His mouth was passionately welded to hers before she could collect her wits. For some reason she had never since been able to rationalise, her lips parted breathlessly and she kissed him with equal fervour, involuntarily and wholeheartedly.

It was he who pulled away suddenly and grasping her shoulders, looked into her face with an expression of profound shock in his hazel eyes.

'You're not Vicky! You must be—Vonne . . .'

Vonne was as shattered as he. Only then did it dawn on her that this was Kirk Leveson, Vicky's fiancé. And she had kissed him—a man she didn't even know—with quite shameful passion.

Her hands flew to her flaming cheeks. 'Oh! I'm sorry . . .' she gasped, overcome with embarrassment. She fled into the house and would have run further still if that would not have caused comment. She couldn't leave Vicky's engagement party. She had to compose herself and try to behave as though nothing had happened.

When Vicky, unaware that they had already met, introduced her sister to Kirk, Vonne caught his eyes and seemed to read there a plea not to mention the encounter on the terrace. She gave her small trembling

hand into the firm grasp of the handsome tow-haired
Australian doctor and pretended there had been no case
of mistaken identity in the garden only minutes before,
but she felt very uncomfortable for the rest of the
evening. Every time she caught Kirk Leveson's gaze an
odd little shiver ran down her spine and she felt his lips
on hers again. She couldn't understand why she had
allowed him to kiss her like that. What must he think of
her!

It was sadly ironic, she now thought, that Kirk, who
had been so anxious to let nothing, not even a trivial
incident like that, hurt Vicky, was now to be deeply
wounded by her.

Vonne's nerves were almost at breaking point when
the plane glided in smoothly and landed at Darwin
airport. She was too agitated to take in much of what she
could see from the window. Her whole mind was con-
centrated on what was about to happen in the next few
minutes.

She saw him before he spotted her. He was half facing
away from her as she approached, which gave her a
moment or two to take in the tall, broad-shouldered,
slim-hipped figure beyond the barrier before he turned
to scan the arriving passengers for the two he had come
to meet.

His tawny hair provided a smooth frame for his
ruggedly chiselled but sensitively delineated profile. He
was standing in the characteristic loose-jointed way she
remembered. In him it was more a mark of self-
possession than of indolence. He was dressed casually
but smartly in a white open-necked coat-style shirt over
brown tailored shorts, and white knee socks, his attire
reflecting the warm climate of this tropical city in the far
north of Australia.

As he caught sight of her, his expression was one of
pleasure mingled with relief, but with an underlying
wariness that startled Vonne. But of course he hadn't

seen Vicky for nearly three months, so probably he was, understandably, a little nervous. Vonne saw with dismay that from his distance he thought she was Vicky.

She came quickly up to him. 'Hello, Kirk.' Her voice trembled and her eyes met his with unspoken apology.

He knew who she was now. He looked puzzled, then alarmed. His eyes flicked around the dispersing crowd expectantly, then darted urgently back to her again, perplexed and demanding.

'Vonne!' he exclaimed, with a sudden tremor in his voice as he added, 'Hello there! Where's Vicky?'

'She—she hasn't come . . .' The words tumbled out. They were not quite the ones she had rehearsed. But there was no way she could delay telling him the truth. He had to know now, right here in this public place with people milling around them. He was bound to guess anyway in a moment.

'Hasn't come? Why? Is she ill?' The hazel eyes were regarding her intently, their warmth fading as suspicion invaded his mind, a suspicion that he was for the moment desperately trying to deny.

Vonne said, 'No, she's not ill—she—she just hasn't come . . .' Her composure almost cracked as a wave of sympathy for him washed over her. She knew only too well what it felt like to be jilted. 'Kirk, I—I can't explain here . . .' She glanced around, trying to convey how unsuitable a place it was to make personal revelations.

He looked at her for a long searching moment. He'd guessed now, and confirmation was stated clearly in her face. Words came into her head but became jumbled in her mouth, and she couldn't speak.

'She's changed her mind, is that it?' A faintly sardonic smile lifted the corners of his mouth.

'Yes, Kirk, I'm sorry . . .' Vonne felt almost as though it were she who was jilting him, not Vicky. It was a cruel joke, she suddenly realised, that she and Vicky were identical twins.

How he must hate me for looking like her but not being Vicky, she thought, dismayed.

'I'm sorry,' she whispered again. 'I've got a letter from her for you . . .' She faltered, her voice fading beneath the onslaught of a gaze that was becoming colder and harder and angrier as the enormity of it sank in.

He moved abruptly to pick up her suitcase and slung her holdall over his shoulder. 'Come on, let's go,' he said in a brisk tone.

If only she knew him better, Vonne thought, she might be better able to cope with the situation. She could feel his withdrawal keenly and knew instinctively that he was not the kind of man to thank her for sympathy, nor turn to her for consolation. She had the uncomfortable feeling that he blamed her as much as Vicky.

When she made an attempt to relieve him of the bulky airline bag as it slipped from his shoulder, as they were leaving the terminal building, he shot her a brief glance and hitched it up again.

'I can manage,' he said in an abrasive tone, and strode on ahead of her.

Vonne trailed disconsolately after him. There was controlled fury in every line of Kirk's large frame, in the way he walked, and the way he left her to follow meekly behind him. But she could hardly have expected him to welcome her, fuss over her, pretend that being jilted was a trivial matter. He had just received a violent shock. His world had been turned upside down. It was only natural that he was angry, with her as well as with Vicky.

She should have told him herself, Vonne thought, and felt guiltily that it was her fault for having let Vicky persuade her to do it instead. I should have insisted, she reproached herself.

She could hardly blame Kirk if he despised her for conspiring with Vicky to deceive him until the last minute. Even the fact that he had been away in Sydney at a seminar for the past week and unreachable was no excuse, she thought now, although she had let Vicky persuade her that it was. Kirk had returned the previous day, and Vicky could have phoned him last night—she should have insisted on that at least. Honouring her contract was one thing, but she shouldn't have become Vicky's emissary.

Outside the airport buildings it was warm and the sunlight was glaring, and the tropical climate and vegetation immediately reminded Vonne of Barbados. She had to walk quickly to keep up with Kirk, who strode towards the car park with long strides despite the burden of her case and bag. Heavy though her luggage was, and she herself had only just managed to struggle through Customs with it, it did not drag down the broad, muscular shoulders. He walked with a straight back and a swinging stride. There was an air of authority about him. He could probably be very arrogant if he chose, Vonne decided. What was it, she wondered, that Armand Saint-Germain had for Vicky that this bronzed Australian did not? She had only met both of them on single occasions, but she felt that if she had been Vicky, and had had to make a choice, she would have preferred Kirk to Armand.

'Hop in!' Kirk's curt command checked her runaway thoughts as they reached his car.

He held open the passenger door of the pale blue Holden Princess. Vonne sank into comfortable sheepskin-covered upholstery and waited while he placed her luggage in the boot. When he slid behind the steering wheel and turned to face her, she felt all her courage draining away once more and she was unable to speak.

His voice had a scalpel edge when he demanded succinctly, 'There's someone else, I presume?'

Vonne was forced to meet the accusing hazel eyes, and she flinched at the smouldering anger in their greeny-gold depths, which could not quite conceal the hurt it was defending. She felt his agony acutely; she had been through it herself.

'I'm afraid so.' With an effort she raised her voice from an apologetic whisper to a matter-of-fact explanatory tone. She must get it over with quickly, for his sake as well as her own. 'She hasn't known him long. He's French, a radiologist at the clinic. They're going to live in Paris.'

'She intends marrying him?' he asked roughly.

'I—I suppose so . . .' Deep colour flooded Vonne's already flushed cheeks. Vicky had been evasive when she'd asked about marriage, but Vonne had assumed that they intended to marry in due course. She did not really approve of Vicky's living with Armand meanwhile, but she had not reproved her. What her sister did was her own business. They did not discuss the intimate details of, or criticise, each other's love-life.

Kirk's mouth twisted and an expression of bitterness narrowed his eyes. 'I see.'

Vonne could not have felt worse if she had been breaking off her own engagement to him. It was just as agonising to have to say on Vicky's behalf, 'It was a mistake, Kirk. She got a bit carried away and thought she was in love with you, but when she met Armand . . .'

'She apparently got carried away even further.' There was contempt in the way he rapped out the words, and in the harsh laugh that accompanied them. 'Lucky Armand!'

In a rush of defensiveness, Vonne said, 'Would you have wanted her to come out here and marry you and regret it?'

Her assertiveness seemed to jolt him. He looked at her with a new, almost apologetic look. 'No, I suppose not,' he conceded. He turned away and stared through the windscreen, his fingers flexing on the steering wheel, betraying his battle to control his emotions.

She fumbled in her handbag and withdrew the letter Vicky had given her for him, and the small wrapped box that contained the engagement ring. She offered them hesitantly. 'Kirk—you'd better have these.'

He did not look at her, nor did he move to take the two items from her. But he was aware, she felt sure, of what she was trying to give him.

'Put them in the glove box,' he ordered curtly, and savagely started the engine. Without speaking, he manoeuvred the car out of the car park.

Vonne said no more about Vicky. She had told him the bare facts; there was nothing she felt she could add at the moment. Perhaps when he had read Vicky's letter and was in a calmer frame of mind, he would want to talk about it again. Maybe then, as Vicky had so badly wanted her to, she could help him to understand—if he would let her. She had a feeling that Kirk was a very different person from Leith. He was not a man to cry on anyone's shoulder—least of all a woman's.

A few minutes later the leaden silence between them lifted briefly. Kirk said, 'I have to call at the hospital first. I hope you don't mind? You needn't put in an appearance yet, though.'

Vonne was puzzled. 'But aren't we going there anyway? I thought the nurses' quarters were in the hospital grounds.'

He answered abruptly, 'The new units aren't finished yet—there's been a delay over materials. It'll be a few weeks yet before they're ready.'

Vonne was taken aback. 'I see. So—where am I staying meanwhile?' she ventured.

Kirk did not have time to answer her question. A car shot out of a side street just ahead of them and swerved to the centre of the road, Kirk braked hard and Vonne was jerked forcefully against the restraining seat-belt. They did not collide with the careering vehicle, but it smashed into a car coming from the opposite direction.

Vonne did not see the moment of impact. She instinctively ducked her head as she was thrust towards the windscreen. She heard the ghastly sounds of metal grinding on metal and the tinkle of glass, and was aware of Kirk's involuntary expletive in unison with her own shrill scream.

CHAPTER TWO

As Vonne slowly raised her head, dazed and shocked, the two cars gave a final shudder, and a deathly silence fell over the scene. Kirk's car had screeched to a halt only a few feet from the crashed vehicles, which were locked in a horrifying embrace in the centre of the road.

The shock that momentarily paralysed them lasted only a few seconds. Vonne could never clearly recall afterwards whether Kirk actually gave any command, or whether it was simply her reflexes that took over, but what she did remember was both of them flinging themselves out of the car and running to the tangled wreckage. People were coming out of nearby houses and other cars were stopping.

A man extricated himself, dazed and bleeding, from the car nearest Vonne. He grabbed her frantically.

'Nadia . . .' he managed to get out hoarsely, 'see to Nadia . . . the baby . . .' and he collapsed at her feet.

Training and experience forced Vonne into professional calm as she dropped to her knees and felt automatically for his pulse, while swiftly running her eyes over him for obvious signs of serious injury. There was, fortunately, no copious bleeding. She guessed he had probably only suffered superficial injuries and shock. He was probably concussed, but at least he was alive.

On the other side of the wrecked cars, Kirk was shouting to someone to call the ambulance. A man in overalls raced up to Vonne and seeing his intention, she said quickly, 'Don't move him until the ambulance comes.' As the man looked doubtfully at the unconscious figure at her feet, she added firmly, 'I'm a nurse. It's just a precaution.'

Then she hurried to the rear of the car which the unconcious man had been driving. She recognised it now as the one that had careered out of control from the side street. Kirk was, she supposed, attending to the occupants of the other car. The rear door was half off its hinges, and in the back seat a woman was moaning.

Vonne leaned in as far as she could and saw a fair-haired girl slumped sideways, half unconscious. There was no baby in the car, but it was obvious that the girl had been on her way to hospital to have one.

'Nadia?' Vonne said gently, squeezing inside as far as the crumpled bodywork of the car would allow. There was a small suitcase jammed between the front and back seats, which made it more difficult. 'Nadia—are you all right?'

There was a trickle of blood oozing from a wound on the girl's head, but Vonne's experienced eye realised that it looked worse than it was. She caught her breath as she realised that something much more urgent required her immediate attention.

Momentarily the girl's head lifted and she gazed at Vonne with shock-glazed and frightened eyes.

'It's coming,' she whimpered, and clutched her distended abdomen, agony distorting the pretty face. With a loud groan as the spasm gripped her, she tried instinctively to spread herself on the seat. Vonne helped to raise her legs and yelled for Kirk. Someone behind her spoke, and she half-turned, thinking it was him, but it wasn't.

Seeing only a stranger, she rapped out, 'Get the doctor—quickly! He's in the other car.'

The face vanished and Vonne turned her attention back to the girl, who was breathing raggedly while tears streamed down her face.

'Adrian—Adrian . . . !' she shrieked in panic at the

onset of fresh pain. 'Where's Adrian?'

'He's all right, love, don't worry, he's all right,' soothed Vonne.

The girl gave a sudden convulsive movement that Vonne recognised as an involuntary physical effort to aid the birth of her child.

'Nadia . . .'

There was no answer. Vonne grasped her wrist and at the same time glanced over her shoulder frantically. Where was Kirk?

In the next few seconds she realised she was going to have to cope alone. She did what she could, which was not very much in the difficult circumstances. She removed the girl's impeding underwear and tried to make her as comfortable as the restricted area permitted. There was little else she could do other than let Nadia clutch her hand till the nails dug painfully into her palm.

Those extraordinary moments remained foggy in her brain, with only fragments of clarity, like the voice of an ambulance man exclaiming, 'Good grief! The woman's giving birth!'

And her own slightly tipsy-sounding voice saying in a wondering tone, 'It's a boy!'

And finally, Kirk's large frame gently easing her aside, taking over with strong hands, reassuring words and an authoritative manner.

'I'm sorry—I couldn't come at once, there was a man bleeding badly. I had to staunch that first.'

Vonne felt warm tears wet her cheeks. Whether she was crying from shock, or joy at having delivered a baby, all on her own, she never knew. She felt an arm around her shoulders, but whether it was Kirk's or one of the ambulance men, did not register.

Gradually the world came back into focus. The baby, damp and wizened, red-faced and protesting loudly, was wrapped in a sheet which one of the ambulance men handed her. 'Here you are, Nurse,' he said, so Kirk or that other man must have told him, she thought. He added, as though he felt she needed reassurance, 'Won't be long. The hospital's just up the road, luckily.'

Vonne rode in the ambulance with Nadia and her baby. Within minutes both were in Casualty and being whisked away by blue-uniformed nurses. Vonne slumped into a chair in the waiting room and waited for Kirk.

A nurse approached, smiling sympathetically. 'You look as though you could do with a cup of tea. You're suffering from shock, I expect. White tea? Sugar?'

'Yes, please, white but no sugar,' said Vonne. She hugged herself to stop the shaking that was suddenly threatening her and changed her mind. 'I think perhaps I will have sugar—I think I need it!'

'Would you like to lie down?' the nurse asked anxiously.

'No—I'm all right,' Vonne insisted. She managed a shaky smile. 'I ought to be—I'm a nurse! But it all happened so quickly, so unexpectedly.'

'Accidents usually do!'

'Was anyone . . . ?' Vonne faltered.

'No, no one killed,' the nurse told her. 'The driver of the other car was taken to Darwin Hospital. He had a bad flesh wound, so Dr Leveson said, but he's in no danger, thanks to prompt action on the Doctor's part.' She smiled. 'And Mrs Laird has a fine son, thanks to you! Just as well you were with Dr Leveson.' She was obviously curious about Vonne but did not ask any personal questions.

Vonne felt weak, and desperately wanted to sleep. She almost did drop off while the nurse was getting her tea, but was jolted back to wakefulness when the girl held out the paper cup.

After a few sips her brain began to function again. 'What hospital is this?' she asked.

'Bauhinia Private,' said the girl, smiling a little quizzically at her ignorance.

Vonne gulped on her tea. 'Bauhinia Private Hospital?' she echoed, and it was her turn to smile. 'Believe it or not, I'm due to start work here soon. I just arrived by plane from London this morning.'

The girl instantly looked interested. 'I thought you sounded English. Well, I'm sure you'll be very welcome here. We're short-staffed as usual.' She pulled a face. 'What an introduction to Darwin for you!' She chuckled. 'I mean, it was hard luck being dragged on duty, so to speak, before you'd hardly arrived.'

A large familiar figure loomed over them and the nurse glanced up. 'Hello, Dr Leveson. You were at work early this morning!' she beamed at him.

His face was still showing strain, but he smiled and, glancing down at Vonne, said, 'You must have a midwifery certificate?'

She shook her head. 'No—I was going to do it when . . .' She broke off. It was hardly the moment to explain how she had come to switch to private nursing instead.

He placed a hand on her shoulder and a peculiar little tremor ran through her. 'You could have fooled me!' There was a fleeting twinkle in his eyes. Vonne felt a calming warmth stealing over her and the shaking stopped. She drank the rest of her tea.

The nurse said, 'Well, I'll be seeing you around, I expect. I'm Jenny Tucker.'

'I'm Vonne Lothian.' Vonne glanced at Kirk with a crooked grin. 'Jenny just told me this is Bauhinia Private Hospital. I suppose I should have realised that right away, as we were on the way here.'

He nodded, and looked hard at her for a moment as though discovering that she was someone else altogether. A flicker of some indefinable emotion passed across his face before he said considerately, 'I think, however, it would be best, as I said before, to leave introducing you to everyone until you've had a chance to unwind. Even more so now.' He drifted a smile in Jenny's direction, saying, 'Your reputation can precede you, courtesy of Nurse Tucker!'

Jenny tossed her head and looked at Kirk with undisguised admiration, and a flirtatious smile. Then she took Vonne's empty cup and left them.

Kirk said, 'We can go now. Everything's under control.' Suddenly the chill was back in his tone, the stoniness in his eyes. Vonne felt as though an arctic wind had spoiled a beautiful summer's day. She followed him out of the hospital. The dramatic episode that had fractured the morning was over. For a short time Kirk had forgotten she had brought hurtful news, but he was remembering now.

Vonne didn't feel like talking, even about the accident, or to enquire where he was taking her now, what sort of accommodation had been arranged for her. He vouchsafed no information himself, and Vonne huddled in her corner of the car, savouring the warm words of praise she had earned from him earlier, and trying not to mind that she might never encounter him in such a mood again. That had been purely professional. Personally, he was bound to keep her at arm's length because of Vicky. She couldn't blame him, but she was disappointed. Kirk Leveson, she had discovered in the past hour or so, was a man she would like to get to know better.

It was not long before they drew up outside a house which was almost totally concealed behind a forest of frangipani, hibiscus, various kinds of palms and cascading bougainvillaea. The neighbouring houses were mostly equally secluded, and it looked to Vonne's eyes like a very well-to-do part of town. She hoped the accommodation would not be too expensive.

'Is this where I'm staying?' she asked tentatively, but Kirk was already getting out of the car and either didn't hear or thought the answer too obvious to be required.

He lifted her luggage out of the boot, then tossed her a key-ring. 'Would you mind opening the front door?'

Vonne walked quickly down the driveway through a tunnel of trees and shrubs, bustling with darting honey-eaters and butterflies, noisy with the chirping of insects. She crossed a wide tiled porch which was attractively furnished with cane chairs flaunting colourful cushions. She pushed the key in the door and flung it open.

Kirk was right behind her. 'Go on in,' he urged impatiently.

Vonne walked into a spacious hallway that led into a huge living-room on one side, and to a wide passage-way on the other.

'Your room is just along the passage,' instructed Kirk. 'Second on the right.'

Vonne paused, anxious to have her curiosity satisfied. 'What's the set-up here, Kirk? Am I in digs or is this a shared house? Who else lives here?' Since it was at present empty, presumably the other occupants were at work.

His eyebrows rose in an expression of astonishment, then he said with a rather humourless smile, 'Oh—I see—Vicky didn't tell you about the delay over the units. They won't be ready for several weeks, I'm afraid. My mother, of course, wouldn't hear of you staying anywhere else but here in the meantime.'

Vonne stared at him, aghast, and felt a wave of anger for her sister. Vicky had surely withheld the information on purpose, afraid it might strengthen Vonne's argu-ments against going. But she couldn't stay here! To have her staying in the same house must be as unthinkable to him, now, as it was to her.

'Kirk, I can't stay here!' she exclaimed.

'Why not?' He did not seem as perturbed as she would have expected.

She shrugged helplessly. 'I can't—I mean, in the

circumstances. It's too—too embarrassing. Besides, you won't want me around. Take me to a hotel, please. I can find somewhere to live until the units are ready, later.'

He regarded her stonily. 'I don't live here. I have my own house. Didn't Vicky tell you that either?'

Perhaps she had in the beginning; Vonne was too confused to remember. She said firmly, 'Kirk, I really do feel terribly embarrassed about this. I—I'd rather go to a hotel. And I'm sure your mother . . .'

'She's expecting you.' His gaze was disconcertingly intense. 'There's no need to change anything. It's not you who's jilted me.' His tone was harsh, his mouth bitter.

But for Vonne, whatever he said, the situation was unbearable.

'I wish I hadn't come,' she said, and to her horror, tears welled up in her eyes. 'I shouldn't have—it was stupid, pointless . . .' She blinked resolutely and faced him stubbornly. 'I think perhaps it would be best if I went straight back home.'

Kirk dumped her holdall on top of her suitcase. He folded his arms and regarded her steadily. Derision coloured his voice as he said, 'Are you saying you want to break your contract before you've even started? Are you as fickle as your sister?'

'That's not fair!' she burst out.

For a long tense moment their eyes locked angrily, no repentance in his, indignation in hers. Finally he looked away and said in a more conciliatory tone, 'It would be a pity, having come so far, if you were to turn around and go straight back. Especially as the hospital needs you. I told John Langham—he's the DN at Bauhinia—what happened this morning but that you weren't in any state for a familiarisation tour, and he's very keen to meet you. He'll be disappointed if you renege now—I dare say he'll expect you to refund your fare.' The look that raked her bordered on contempt.

And suddenly it was important that he should not think she was a girl who did not honour commitments, that she was unreliable and didn't care whom she disrupted or let down. He had arranged the job for her, and it would reflect badly on his judgment if she proved a non-starter. He was suffering enough because of Vicky. She didn't want him to suffer, even in the slightest, because of her.

Vonne bit her lip. 'I just thought . . .'

'Forget it,' he said brusquely, and picked up her luggage again. 'Your room is just along the passage,' he said, 'second on the right.'

Vonne walked along to it. The door was ajar and she pushed it wide open. Kirk dumpled her suitcase on the floor and crossed to open the venetian blind at the windows. Vonne glanced around the room, receiving an instant impression of cheerful comfort and elegant good taste. She noticed with a pang the twin beds, meant of course for her and Vicky.

Kirk paused on his way out. 'If you want to shower and change, the bathroom's next door.' His eyes travelled swiftly over her crumpled, soiled dress and torn tights. There were bloodstains on both as well as streaks of grease and dirt. He added, 'I'll be in the kitchen. I expect you'd like something to eat.'

Vonne protested, 'Please don't bother—you must be busy.'

She received an ironic smile. 'Not today. Naturally I took a day off to meet my fiancée.'

Vonne wished she hadn't made the remark. It was just a painful reminder to him.

'Thank you,' she said. There was no point in being churlish. He was doing his best to be courteous in a difficult situation, although he must be anxious to get away from her. How desperately he must want to be alone after what had happened!

A short time later, showered and changed into one

of the pastel print cotton sundresses she had bought in Barbados, feeling they would also be perfect for Darwin's climate, she felt considerably refreshed. She did not bother with make-up, merely shaped her naturally arching dark eyebrows and wiped a touch of lip gloss on her healthily glowing lips. The tan she had acquired in Barbados was smoother and more golden than most girls with red in their colouring could achieve. She did not tan easily or quickly, but the month in the Caribbean sun had allowed her to nurture an even tan slowly. The only blemishes were a few attractive freckles on her nose.

Kirk was not in the kitchen. Vonne peeped into the adjoining sun-room which was resplendent with tropical plants and ferns and coolly decorated in pastel greens and yellows. He was not there either. Vonne dawdled uncertainly, her eyes running over the lacquered pine table, set with fine white china on a green tablecloth. In one corner of the room a Japanese wind-chime tinkled musically in the light breeze filtering through a narrow louvred window above double glass doors which opened on to a lush garden. In the centre of the patio outside a fountain splashed and sparkled in filtered sunlight. Vonne's attention was drawn to a honey-eater darting in and out of a flowering shrub and she was watching it, fascinated, as it probed the flowers for nectar when a door slammed, startling her.

Kirk joined her. He looked her over with slow deliberation, but his lingering gaze revealed nothing of his thoughts. When his eyes reached hers there was only chill withdrawal in the tawny depths.

'You were quick,' he said in a flat tone.

'Your mother has a very beautiful garden,' Vonne remarked, dragging her eyes away from his, and wishing there was some magic she could perform to ease his pain.

'She's a gardening fanatic,' Kirk answered with a

smile that showed warmth of affection. 'How do you like your coffee? Milk and sugar?'

'Just milk, thank you.'

He went back to the kitchen and quickly reappeared with two mugs of coffee which he carried into the sun-room and placed on a small table between two large cane armchairs.

Vonne sat in one and reached for her mug of coffee. Kirk did not sit, but picked up his mug and stood with his back to the window a few paces away. Since Vonne was facing the light she could not see his features clearly which made her feel considerably at a disadvantage.

At last she said, 'I appreciate how difficult this is for you, Kirk, and I do wish you wouldn't feel so— so obliged to be hospitable. Why don't you just leave me . . .' She didn't know how to finish.

He ignored her suggestion and said, 'It really is quite uncanny how alike you and Vicky are.'

'We are identical twins,' she reminded him.

'Not quite identical,' he said, as though just discovering it. 'There are differences, I'm sure.'

Vonne made light of it. 'Well, we do tend to wear a different style of clothes.'

Kirk gave a short laugh. 'Rebellion against being dressed identically when you were little?'

'Partly, I suppose. But our personalities are not as identical as our looks.'

There was a lengthy silence during which, although she looked everywhere but at him, Vonne was conscious of his eyes on her. She had the uncomfortable feeling that he was willing her to turn into Vicky, and that he could not quite accept that she wasn't.

She searched desperately for something to say and at last came up with the obvious. 'Where is your mother, Kirk? Does she work?'

'Yes. She's a pharmacist. She has a shop in town.'

Even as he spoke, Vonne recalled Vicky mentioning

it, ages ago when they were first engaged, but she had been too preoccupied with her own affairs then, and Leith, to retain the details.

She said, 'Yes, I remember now. Vicky did say something about that . . .' and was stopped by the unfathomable look in his eyes.

'If it hadn't been for the accident, we would have been here for breakfast,' Kirk commented. 'She was sorry she had to go in today. Normally she would have left her manageress to cope, but Phyllis is away ill at the moment. She'll be home around six, I expect.'

'It's very kind of her to have me here.'

He did not answer, and Vonne felt disinclined to ask too many more questions. She felt too uneasy with him and feared he would resent it.

After another lengthy silence, he said, 'Is there anything else you want to tell me—anything else Vicky wanted you to tell me?'

Vonne's mind seemed to have gone blank. She wasn't really making much of a job of helping him to understand Vicky's change of heart, she thought. 'No—no, I don't think so,' she said falteringly. She wondered if he had read Vicky's letter yet. Probably he had done so while she was in the shower. She said, 'Vicky's not very good at writing letters. That's why she wanted me to tell you—in case she hadn't put it very well, I suppose.' It all seemed so futile now. Vonne swallowed hard and said desperately, 'Don't be too hard on her, Kirk. She couldn't help falling in love with Armand. And she was terribly distraught at the thought of hurting you. Please try to believe that. She didn't want to do it—she was desperate for me to assure you of that. She didn't want you to think she was just flippant . . . Kirk, if you'd seen her . . .'

'I'd probably have wrung her pretty little neck!' he said with a depth of feeling that was echoed in a bitter little laugh. He went on harshly, 'I don't care much for people who get others to do their dirty work for them. The least she could have done was to have phoned me and explained.'

'You were in Sydney all last week at that seminar,' Vonne excused quickly, 'and she only realised she couldn't go through with it because of Armand a few days before we were due to leave. It was very difficult for her to have to make a decision at the last minute like that.'

'I would have telephoned her from Sydney before you left,' he mused grimly, 'but I was tied up the whole time.' He added scathingly, 'I wonder if she would have had the guts to tell me if I had, or would she have pretended everything was OK?'

Vonne protested that she didn't think Vicky would have been that much of a coward, but she didn't really know. She wondered if, Vicky having confessed, Kirk would still have insisted that Vonne honour her contract with the hospital. She thought probably not. It was only now that she was actually here that he wanted to hold her to it.

A clock chimed midday and Kirk drained his coffee mug. 'We might as well eat,' he said, and reaching for her mug, 'Another coffee?'

Vonne rose protestingly. 'Kirk, you don't have to . . .' How could she sit through a meal with him knowing he was antagonistic towards her yet duty bound to be polite? 'Kirk I'm sure you'd rather leave me here, and I shan't mind in the least if you do. Just tell me where things are and I'll get myself some lunch.'

His fingers closed around hers briefly in the transference of her mug to him. His hand was cool, a smooth, soft surgeon's hand, but firm and infinitely capable, she was sure. She had felt that when he had touched her shoulder earlier at the hospital, and now the same tingling warmth surged through her like an electric current. She withdrew her hand quickly, and he clashed the delicate china mugs together rather clumsily.

He said, 'There's no need—Mother left lunch for us. It's all ready. She'll be disappointed if we don't eat it.'

He had not, however, responded to the first part of her remark. She tried again. 'I meant you don't have to stay because you feel you have to be polite to me,' she said awkwardly. 'I know how painful it must be for you, and I'm terribly sorry—I'd quite understand.'

'Oh, for God's sake,' he suddenly flared, 'stop being so damned sanctimonious about it! I don't want your sympathy or your understanding. In fact I don't want to talk about it. OK?'

Vonne recoiled at his vehemence and sank back in the chair as though he had shoved her. She said nothing, feeling that whatever she said now would only make matters worse. He gave her no chance to, in any case, because he stalked abruptly out of the room. A moment or two later he came back and thrust her refilled coffee mug into her hand, although she had not actually said she wanted it.

'Won't be long,' he said, without looking at her, and when she asked if she could help, his answer was a curt, 'No.'

Vonne stood at the window and looked out into the garden, so peaceful with its lush vegetation, flitting birds and butterflies, the rhythmic splashing of the fountain into the pool, and the lazily circling goldfish. But the scene outside could not soothe her agitation or relax the tension between her and Kirk.

When she moved across to the table at his brisk invitation and sat down, she saw that Mrs Leveson had gone to a great deal of trouble to provide a tempting lunch. Kirk sat opposite her, and she was uncomfortably aware of the unused place-setting alongside him which he had not removed. Had he left it in order to discomfit her, or was he merely tormenting himself?

As she toyed with lettuce leaves and slices of cucumber dipped in yoghurt, and savoured the delicious smooth flesh of avocado sprinkled with a French dressing, which she scarcely had any appetite for, Vonne wished all over again that she had stayed in England.

It might not have mattered so much if she had been able to go straight to the nurses' quarters, but having to stay here was so embarrassing. What would his mother think? Surely she would be as hostile as Kirk. No mother relishes her son's being jilted. She would see Vonne as a party to deception, as Kirk obviously did. She might, as he was doing, pretend otherwise out of politeness, but it would be a strain. Too great a strain, Vonne decided. She would definitely move out and go to a hotel tomorrow. She dared not, however, voice this intention again to Kirk.

'When am I expected to start work?' she ventured after a long chilly silence.

'As soon as you feel up to it,' he answered briefly. 'I could drive you over to see John tomorrow if you like. Let me know later.'

'I'd like to buy a car as soon as I can,' Vonne said.

He agreed with a nod but offered no suggestions. Vonne noticed that he was not eating much either. She tried to do a little better justice herself to the meal his mother had so generously prepared, but it was an effort. Every morsel of food seemed to stick in her throat.

She was relieved when Kirk said, 'I expect you're suffering from jet-lag despite your stopover in Singapore, especially with this morning's drama on top of it. You might as well rest this afternoon. I called Mother to tell her about the accident.'

And that Vicky didn't come, thought Vonne, wishing yet again that there was some way she could help him come to terms with it.

She pushed her chair back and started to collect the plates. 'I'll clear away and wash up,' she said, giving him the signal for prompt departure.

He followed her out to the kitchen. 'Just stack them in the dishwasher,' he told her, and indicated the machine under a pale green formica worktop.

He left her then, without any further conversation. Vonne felt a wave of relief when she heard the front door close behind him. She had just spent, she felt, the most agonising morning of her whole life.

With a deep sigh, she took the tablecloth outside to shake it. She was folding it, still standing at the back door, looking down the garden, when the full force of jet-lag hit her. It was like being clouted with something very solid, and she almost staggered.

She left the folded tablecloth on the kitchen worktop since she was not sure where to put it. Then she went along to her room and collapsed on the bed. In seconds she was dead to the world, and she did not stir again for several hours.

CHAPTER THREE

WHEN Vonne woke she could hear piano music faintly, but could not tell whether someone in the house was playing an instrument or whether it was a recording or the radio. She lay listening for a few minutes, still in a semi-conscious state.

Slowly the events of the day came back, crowding her mind and reminding her of the impossible situation she was in. The piano music, whatever its origin, suggested that Kirk's mother must be at home. Vonne looked at her watch, but it had stopped. She had fogotten to wind it.

She slowly raised herself to sit on the edge of the bed. She still felt lethargic, as though her head was stuffed with cotton wool. What she needed was another reviving shower. But first, perhaps she should let Mrs Leveson know she was awake.

Hurriedly running a comb through her tangled curls, she ventured out. Kirk's mother was in the sun-room reading a newspaper, a brandy glass cradled in one slender hand. The music emanated from a concealed stereo.

Vonne's bare feet made no sound on the soft carpet and Mrs Leveson was so absorbed in her newspaper she did not notice her, which gave Vonne a moment or two to take in the woman who was Kirk's mother.

Mrs Leveson was small and pretty, with sleek blonde hair swept into an elegant coil at the back of her head. Her skin was a milky brown, and Vonne thought she had never seen such smooth, long slender legs on a woman of her age, which must be past fifty. Her profile was towards Vonne and there was a strong resemblance to

Kirk in it. They had the same shaped nose and slight tilt
to the eyes, the same square, determined chin, but what
was rugged in Kirk was almost fragile in his mother.
Kirk's physique, Vonne decided, must have come from
his father.

'Mrs Leveson . . .'

Vonne's soft voice startled the older woman, and the
newspaper rustled to the floor as she looked up. Her face
broke into a smile that gave no hint of what her true
feelings must be.

'My dear—you gave me a start!' Instantly she un-
crossed her elegant bare legs and moved gracefully with
her hand extended towards Vonne.

There were laughter lines at the corners of her eyes,
like Kirk's, but her eyes were a deep violet blue, and
although they were totally without hostility, Vonne
was aware that she was being appraised with shrewd
thoroughness.

'I'm sorry.' Vonne smiled and clasped the outstretched hand. 'I just flaked out after lunch, I'm
afraid—jet-lag, I suppose. I didn't hear you come home.
Is it very late—I'm afraid my watch has stopped.'

Mrs Leveson's firm grasp belied her fragile appearance. Her eyes rested with curiosity on Vonne's face. 'So
you're Vonne,' she said musingly. A swift shadow
erased her smile and she continued a little tensely, 'I
could hardly believe it when Kirk told me what had
happened.' She sighed. 'Poor boy! It must have been a
dreadful shock.'

'I know—and I'm terribly sorry,' said Vonne. She
rushed on, 'I shouldn't have come—I've made it worse.
I shouldn't have let Vicky persuade me . . .' She broke
off. It wasn't entirely Vicky's fault.

Mrs Leveson said kindly, 'I'm not sure that you have
made it worse.' She did not explain the remark and her
smile slid back as she continued, 'You really are very like
Vicky, aren't you? Kirk showed me a photograph of

your sister. He said it's quite uncanny and I'd have trouble telling you apart at first.'

'It does take a while to get to know us,' Vonne admitted. 'Although we dress differently, which helps.'

Mrs Leveson's eyes twinkled. 'I used to wish I had an identical twin when I was a child. I thought it would be such fun to fool people!'

Vonne blushed at the memory of doing just that, many times. 'It can be. We used to fool our teachers all the time, and sometimes even our parents, but we couldn't fool them for long.'

Mrs Leveson's laughter was warm and vibrant. Vonne, to her surprise, felt instantly at ease with her. Kirk's mother said, 'I only arrived home about half an hour ago. I usually unwind with a drink while I read the paper, which I never have time for in the mornings. Would you like a drink, Vonne?'

Vonne declined. 'I'd rather have a shower first, if I may. I need waking up!'

'Of course, my dear. Go ahead. Please make yourself at home, Vonne. Come back when you're ready—I'm dying to hear all about this morning's little drama. All Kirk said was that you rose to the occasion splendidly.'

She added, 'Would you feel up to going out to dinner tonight? It would save a lot of bother.'

Vonne was still gulping at Kirk's praise, and savouring it. She said, 'Er—yes—if you'd rather . . .' then she felt she must announce her intentions straight away, so she said, 'It's very kind of you to have me here, Mrs Leveson, but I really think it would be better if tomorrow I found somewhere else to live until the units are finished.'

Mrs Leveson frowned, and looked perplexed. 'Somewhere else? Why?'

Vonne explained. Kirk's mother gave an imperious wave of her hand and dismissed the idea. 'Nonsense,' she said with emphasis. 'I've been looking forward to having a couple of young girls in the house. My own daughters went south and got married and I seldom see them these days.' She considered Vonne again. 'You're about Margaret's age, I think. Twenty-four?'

'I'm nearly twenty-five, actually.'

Mrs Leveson gave her a long considering look, then said, 'Run along and have your shower, and we'll talk it over later.' As Vonne was going she added, 'Do call me Diana.'

A short while later, Vonne reappeared in a pale green linen-look dress with a finely pleated skirt, pintucked bodice and matching short-sleeved jacket.

'How delicious you look!' Diana Leveson exclaimed. She laughed. 'I know how you're feeling. I always feel dreadful after a long flight, even if I scrupulously avoid alcohol and do all the things I'm supposed to do.'

She had changed too, from the smart businesslike dark blue skirt and striped shirt she had been wearing, into a simply styled lilac shirtwaister dress.

'We might as well go out straight away,' she said, 'and then you can have an early night. By tomorrow you'll be back to normal, I expect.'

Diana chatted in a friendly way all the way into town, telling Vonne about Darwin and promising to take her sightseeing. It seemed, Vonne thought once, as though she was deliberately trying to counter her son's unfortunate but understandable antagonism.

The restaurant she took Vonne to was a small friendly place where she was evidently a regular customer. The waiter who welcomed them looked Vonne over with curiosity and a gleam of admiration in his eyes. He ushered them to a secluded booth and left them to study the menu.

As soon as they had ordered, Diana reopened the conversation at the point they had left it earlier in the evening, and which Vonne felt she had deliberately avoided on the way.

She said candidly, 'Let's get one thing straight, Vonne. There's no need for you to feel awkward about staying with me. I understand your feelings and I sympathise, but it's not for me to judge either Vicky or you. I am very disappointed for Kirk, and a little angry too, I admit, but I'm inclined to think it must be for the best. Naturally he's upset, but time will heal the hurt. It always does.'

'I suppose so,' Vonne agreed. She wasn't sure time would ever heal the hurt she had suffered over Leith, however. And she couldn't help wondering if Kirk's suffering would fester like her own.

'Besides,' said Diana reasonably, 'it will only be a short while before you can move into one of the new units. Since we'd got everything ready for you and Vicky, it would seem silly for you to go elsewhere.'

Vonne did not want to appear ungrateful. She battled with herself for a moment, while Diana smiled encouragingly. At last, with a little sigh, she said, 'Well, all I can say, Diana, is you're being extraordinarily generous and understanding.'

'Rubbish,' scoffed Diana. 'Now let's agree that it's settled, shall we?'

After a moment she said, 'Fortunately, only a few people know Kirk became engaged while he was in England. John Langham—the DN at the Bauhinia—knew, of course, because Kirk arranged your job with him. He and Kirk are close friends, besides. I doubt if anyone else at the hospital knew. Kirk has always been very close about his private life.' She smiled a little sadly. 'He was looking forward to surprising everyone when Vicky arrived. Which was just as well, as it turns out. He would hate being gossiped about. It's not very nice being jilted and worse when everyone knows about it.'

'Yes, it's horrible,' said Vonne with a little sigh.

Diana picked up the emotion in her voice. 'You've been through it too?' she asked, surprised.

Vonne nodded, and stupidly her eyes filled with tears. She hadn't meant to talk about Leith; she just wanted to forget. But suddenly she found herself telling Diana about him. Kirk's mother listened with sympathy, nodding from time to time as Vonne briefly described what had happened.

'It must have been ghastly for you,' Diana said at last, adding with genuine feeling, 'I do hope getting right away as you have will help.' Then she asked, 'Does Kirk know?'

'I don't think so. I doubt that Vicky would have mentioned it without asking me if she could. She'd know I wouldn't have wanted to be offered a job out of sympathy.' Vonne pleaded anxiously, 'I'd rather you didn't tell him . . .'

'I wouldn't dream of it,' said Diana. 'It's your personal affair.' She went on in a lighter tone, 'So Barbados is how you achieved your wonderful sun-tan! I dare say you won't find life here quite so exotic, but at least the climate is similar.'

Vonne was glad to talk about something else. 'It's all very exciting for me,' she said, 'just because it isn't England. I've never worked away from home before, and going to Barbados was the first time I'd been abroad.'

Diana was amused. 'Funny, isn't it? I've lived in the Top End most of my life, to me it's home. Everything is so familiar I can hardly imagine that it could be exotic to outsiders!'

'Don't you ever feel cut off being so far from the other cities?' queried Vonne.

Diana shrugged, thought about it and said, 'Not really. I was born here. When I went to university in Adelaide I hated it. I couldn't wait to come back. Luckily Bill, my late husband, whom I met down there, was a Top Ender too. He was at med. school and I was doing pharmacy. Since we both wanted to come back to Darwin, there was no argument!'

She went on, 'Kirk's like me, he's a Territory man. He couldn't get back fast enough. He spent a long time down south getting qualified, as you would guess, but he never became conditioned to the southern environment. He always wanted to come back. Actually, even Darwin is a bit urban for him. He's a true Outback man under the skin. Bill used to say he should have been a Flying Doctor—you know, the air ambulance service that serves the people who live in isolated areas?'

'Yes, I've heard quite a lot about it,' said Vonne, fascinated by this fleshing out of Kirk. Vicky had told her only sketchy details about the man she intended to marry. There hadn't been much opportunity with Vonne being away in Cornwall, and then Barbados. It occurred to Vonne now that perhaps part of the trouble was that Vicky had not had time to get to know Kirk terribly well herself.

'He gets away whenever he can,' Diana went on. 'We have a cattle station. It's been in the family for generations—Kirk's great-grandfather was one of the early pioneers. The station's a hundred miles south of Darwin. You must come with us to Walparoo some time,' she insisted with enthusiasm. 'But first we must make sure you see Darwin and some of the sights round about. Darwin is a very modern city now. There's been a tremendous amount of rebuilding since Tracy . . .'

'Tracy?'

'Cyclone Tracy. You may have heard about it. It struck Darwin on Christmas Eve 1974 and all but obliterated the town.'

'I remember,' Vonne said. 'It was in all the newspapers and on television at home. The scenes of devastation were horrifying.'

She must have looked anxious because Diana said, 'Don't worry, it's rare for one so fierce to hit us, and even if another Tracy does blow up, we're much better prepared for it. The new buildings are more cyclone-proof.

Bauhinia Hospital, for instance, would need a cyclone ten times the power of Tracy to wreck it.'

'It's a fairly new hospital, isn't it?' said Vonne.

'Very new. It was only built a couple of years ago. We've had a big increase in population in recent times. A lot of people whose homes were wrecked in the cyclone never came back, but there've been plenty and more to replace them. By the way, when do you expect to start work at the Bauhinia?'

'As soon as I can,' said Vonne with a smile. 'I've been rather a long time away from the wards and I'm keen to get back as soon as I can.'

'Did you see John Langham today?' Diana enquired.

'No. Kirk said he'd take me along tomorrow, but we didn't make a definite arrangement . . .' Vonne said doubtfully. 'Actually there's no need to bother him. I know how busy he must be.'

'I'm sure he wants to be bothered,' said Diana firmly. 'He arranged for you to work there. I'll give him a call tonight and see what he intends to do.'

Vonne saw that it would be useless to argue. Diana was as single-minded as her son when she made up her mind about something.

Diana went on conversationally, 'You've arrived at the best time of year. This is what we call the Dry, which lasts until about the end of September. It's not as humid as in the Wet—which is what we call summer here. That's when it rains—really rains. None of your soft English drizzle here! This is the tropics and it buckets down. The temperature though rarely falls below thirty centigrade all year round. You won't need winter clothes up here.'

'That's what Vicky said, so I didn't bring any,' Vonne confessed with a laugh. 'Just a few cardigans.'

'Yes, you'll need those. It can get quite cool by comparison in the evenings.'

They lingered over the meal talking until Vonne

suddenly yawned and Diana said it was time they went home.

While Vonne was getting ready for bed, Diana telephoned Kirk, then relayed the message that he would call for Vonne after breakfast in the morning if she felt up to it. If she wanted to have a couple of days' complete rest, that was quite all right, Diana said. Vonne guessed that was Diana's idea rather than Kirk's. She said she didn't think she needed to. An interview with the DN wasn't likely to be strenuous.

As she was anxious not to keep Kirk waiting in the morning, Vonne set her little travelling alarm clock for an early hour to be sure that she was up and dressed well before breakfast. Kirk arrived as they were clearing the breakfast table and stacking plates in the dishwasher.

His mother offered him coffee, but he was in too much of a hurry. 'I've got a heavy schedule today,' he said. 'Surgery this morning and I'm operating this afternoon. A full list, so I'll be late, I expect.'

His eyes drifted over Vonne, lazily absorbing the simple short-sleeved blue dress she was wearing and then lingering rather thoughtfully on her face. Vonne nervously fingered the fine strand of tiny white shells around her neck.

'Ready?' The abrupt query made her jump.

'Yes.' She picked up her white handbag which was lying on a chair.

'Don't let John make a slave out of her,' Diana chided. 'Just because she's willing!'

Kirk's eyes burned momentarily into Vonne's. 'I'm afraid she'll have to stand up for herself,' he said. 'I don't run the hospital.'

He bent and kissed Diana's proffered cheek, and she patted him affectionately. 'Have a good day, both of you.' To Vonne she said, 'Do make yourself at home when you get back. There's plenty of food in the fridge and pantry cupboard.'

Vonne thanked her and mentally decided that she would cook the evening meal, as Diana was bound to come home tired and would surely appreciate it. It was a small thing she could do to show her gratitude.

On the way to the hospital, Vonne asked a few questions about it, and Kirk answered in tones which discouraged her from pursuing points. He was in no mood for talking, that was clear. And he was only accompanying her, she knew, because he felt obliged to, having been responsible for getting her the job, and for holding her to the arrangement.

How long would it take for him to get over loving her sister? she wondered. She had thought she was getting over Leith while she was in Barbados, but the minute she returned, the pain was as sharp as ever. Perhaps the wounds were too deep ever to heal. Had Vicky wounded Kirk as deeply? Vicky felt a sudden rush of anger at her sister, anger even greater than that she had felt towards Leith for hurting her.

Vonne had not really taken in much of the hospital on the previous day, but now she saw that it was a modern, pastel green building with clean lines, three stories high and surrounded by pleasant well-kept lawns edged by shrubberies and flower beds. A line of fan-shaped travellers' palms flanked the entrance, and there were clumps of banana palms beyond them. Pink flowering shrubs grew against the walls and were called bauhinias or butterfly bushes, Kirk told her briefly, because of their winglike leaves.

Sprinklers swept a glittering spray across the lawns, and the flower-beds were vivid with colour. Vonne was delighted when a large black and white bird with a long curved beak strutted across the grass as they drove into the car-park.

'What is it?' she asked eagerly.

'A straw-necked ibis. You'll see a lot of them around,' Kirk informed her briefly.

He took her straight to the Director of Nursing's office. John Langham was expecting them. He was a burly ginger-haired man with a florid complexion and a broad smile. He grabbed Vonne's hand in a hard, welcoming handshake and invited her to sit down.

'Delighted to welcome you to the staff,' he said, and turning to Kirk, 'Eh, Kirk?' There was a preoccupied look in Kirk's eyes as he nodded. John Langham went on, 'You passed your first test with flying colours yesterday, so Kirk told me.'

Vonne blushed. She didn't dare look at Kirk. He said abruptly, 'If you don't mind, John, I'll leave Vonne with you. I'm rather busy this morning.'

'No worries, Kirk,' the DN said amiably. 'We'll look after Nurse Lothian, don't worry.'

Before Vonne could thank him for bringing her, Kirk had gone, relieved no doubt to escape.

'Let's have some coffee.' John Langham pressed a button on his intercom and ordered it. He leaned back in his swivel chair, hands clasped across his rather ample stomach, and regarded Vonne with interest, and a candidly approving eye. He asked about her trip out, then invited her to outline her career so far.

Vonne told him where she had trained and how, after obtaining her SRN certificate, she had continued to work at the same hospital until, persuaded by the mother of a patient she was nursing, she had taken a private nursing post temporarily. She did not of course mention the disastrous outcome of that interlude.

'But you did your midwifery?' he prompted.

Vonne shook her head. 'No. I was going to, but I took on this private nursing job instead. I have nursed in labour and maternity wards, though.'

'Good. You'll get plenty of practice in every aspect of general nursing here, Vonne. We're not a large hospital and we, like just about everyone else, have staffing problems. Nurses here become very much Jills of all trades. Any theatre experience?'

'A little.'

'Good. Our operating rooms are always in need of extra assistance when there's a rush on.'

The coffee arrived and he broke off his questions about nursing to ask, 'Milk and sugar?'

Vonne declined both.

'Slimming? You don't look as though you need to!' He had a warm smile and his easy-going manner put her at ease. 'I'm afraid I like plenty of milk and sugar.' He added them lavishly to his cup and Vonne thought it was hardly any wonder he was rather corpulent. He was around forty-five, she judged, the age to be taking a little more care of his heart.

Stirring his cup vigorously, he said, 'I don't want to rush you, Vonne, but when could you start? Unfortunately, we've got several staff off sick at the moment —there's been a 'flu bug going around—so we're having a bit of a problem stretching the rosters.'

'I can start straight away,' Vonne volunteered at once. 'Tomorrow, if you like.'

He viewed her considerately. 'Wouldn't you like a day or two to acclimatise?'

Vonne saw that he was hoping she would say no, so she did. 'No, I'm quite anxious to get back to work,' she said.

He didn't argue. 'Splendid! We'll put you on a day shift for a start, but I presume you won't mind doing nights when necessary?'

'Not at all.'

He drained his cup and rose. 'That's very satisfactory, then. Now, shall we take a walk around? I'll introduce you to a few of the people you'll be working with. Sister Kent probably needs an extra pair of hands most at the moment, so we'll finish up there—she's in charge of the gynae wards.' He gave Vonne an encouraging pat on the shoulder as he came around the desk and she rose. 'I hope you'll enjoy working with us, Vonne,' he said warmly. 'I'm sure you'll fit in splendidly.'

'I hope so.'

His face was sober for a moment. 'It's a shame about Kirk and your sister.'

'Yes, it is.'

He shrugged. 'These things happen. That's life, I suppose. I guess Kirk won't be too keen to get involved with a woman again for a while.'

As though to put a full stop to the subject, he held open the door and ushered Vonne through.

There were no operations in progress, so Vonne was able to see over the theatre complex as well as other parts of the hospital. She quickly realised that it was a very up-to-date hospital. On their progress through the wards, most of which were three, four or five-bed rooms, Vonne was immediately struck by the atmosphere of casual friendliness and the absence of the kind of austere formality still to be found in some larger hospitals.

Finally the DN took her to an office on the first floor. 'Now, to introduce you to Sister Kent,' he said.

The office was empty. He stopped a passing nurse. 'Is Lorin around?'

'She was a minute ago,' the girl said, and as light footsteps sounded on the vinyl tiles behind them, 'Here she is.'

A tall, dark-haired girl with a voluptuous figure that was accentuated more than disguised by her uniform approached. She smiled at John Langham and treated Vonne to curious appraisal.

'You were looking for me, Mr Langham?' she queried.

'Yes, Sister. I've brought you a new member of staff.' He pushed open the office door, standing aside for Vonne and Sister Kent to go in. They all sat down, Sister Kent behind the small formica-topped desk. Vonne found she was a subject of close scrutiny from Sister

Kent's rather cold blue eyes.

The DN introduced Vonne, explaining, 'She's the SRN Kirk persuaded to join us when he was in the UK a few months back.' Vonne wondered if this simplification was his or Kirk's.

'Really?' Sister Kent's eyes flashed surprise, and a trace of annoyance because she had not been made aware of it before.

John Langham went on, 'Vonne was keen to work abroad for a while, so he snapped her up for us. As you're running on a skeleton staff at the moment, she'd better start with you. It'll help to ease your roster a bit. She's willing to start straight away, tomorrow if you like.'

Sister Kent looked neither pleased nor grateful; instead, her look was almost unfriendly. As the DN finished speaking, the beeper in his jacket pocket signalled insistently. He backed towards the door. 'I'll leave Vonne with you, Lorin.' To Vonne he said, 'Pop back and see me before you go. There are a few details I need from you.'

There was an uncomfortable silence after he had gone. Sister Kent considered Vonne speculatively, and Vonne's heart sank a little. Everyone else had been so welcoming.

Sister Kent said finally, 'So you're from England? What made you think you would enjoy nursing in the Top End?' Her tone suggested it was doubtful she would.

'I was keen to try a new experience,' Vonne said carefully.

The senior nurse smiled meaningfully. 'I hope Dr Leveson wasn't the main attraction.'

Vonne was glad she was able to answer truthfully, 'Not at all.' A faint flush of indignation at the suggestion suffused her cheeks and she saw with some chagrin that Sister Kent probably did not believe her.

'Where did you meet him?'

'At a party. A friend of my sister's is an Australian nurse. Sylvia often has visiting Australian medicos staying with her, or at parties.'

Sister Kent continued her cool assessment of Vonne for a moment or two, then laughed disparagingly. 'Well, if you've had any secret dreams of snaring poor Kirk, I'm afraid you'll be very disappointed.' She paused, then added casually, 'I think you'll find he's already committed.'

There was something in her tone that convinced Vonne that she did not know about Vicky, and that she was referring to herself, perhaps with the same wishful thinking she had attributed to Vonne. In which case, Vonne was thinking in alarm, she could regard me as a rival.

After another long piercing glance, Sister Kent asked Vonne a few questions about her experience, and then rising from the desk offered the brisk advice, 'Well, the first thing you'll have to learn is that we do a lot of things differently here.'

Without thinking, Vonne said, 'What, for instance?' She hadn't meant it to, but even to her own ears it sounded truculent. The other nurse's manner was making her feel that way.

Lorin Kent stiffened in annoyance, and her mouth thinned. She placed slender hands on slender hips and treated her new nurse to a scathing look.

'Not being rude to seniors, for a start!' she snapped.

'I'm sorry . . .' Vonne really was. She had not meant to sound rude. It was just that the unfriendly vibes she was experiencing had aggravated her. She knew a deep misgiving. The sharp exchange hardly boded well for a good working relationship. She was definitely starting off on the wrong foot.

Sister Kent enquired casually, 'Where are you staying?'

Even before she spoke, Vonne realised that her
answer would not please, but she could hardly lie. 'I'm
staying with Dr Leveson's mother at the moment,' she
admitted. 'I'm supposed to be having one of the new
units when they're completed.'

Sister Kent gave an indulgent little laugh. 'Oh dear,
poor Kirk! He's such a soft touch, so easily persuaded to
do a good deed.' Her tone hardened. 'But don't imagine
that just because you twisted him around your little
finger to get you a job here, that will give you any special
privileges. Just because he's taken you under his wing
temporarily it doesn't mean he'll want you living in his
pocket.'

'I most certainly don't expect to!' retorted Vonne,
resenting the tone of the girl's remarks, and resentful of
the accusation. 'And I certainly didn't twist him around
my little finger, as you put it! I understood that an
addition to the nursing staff would be more than welcome here! In fact, everyone else has made me *feel* very
welcome.' Her usually gentle eyes flashed with indignation. 'If you don't believe me, ask Kirk—and then I
think you'll find you owe me an apology!'

The Charge Sister's eyes narrowed dangerously and
her lips puckered in extreme annoyance. 'If you want to
nurse here, this is hardly the way to begin. You'd better
learn to keep a civil tongue in your head *before* you
commence your duties!'

Vonne could have kicked herself. Demanding an
apology from a senior was something she would never
normally have contemplated, even under stress, but
Lorin Kent had riled her more than anyone she could
remember.

She drew a long slow breath, and with as much
deference as she could muster, muttered, 'I'm sorry,
Sister.' But she could not help saying defensively, 'If you
would prefer not to have me on your wards, then
perhaps we should refer to Mr Langham.'

Which will probably mean I'll be sacked before I even start, Vonne thought ruefully. John Langham wouldn't want a troublemaker on the staff, and that was how Sister Kent would surely present her. What would Kirk say? she wondered. And Diana? It was too horrible to contemplate.

There was a stony silence while the two girls, the senior nurse not much older than Vonne, regarded each other. They were about the same height, and their eyes were almost level as for a few tense seconds the battle of wills raged silently on.

At last Sister Kent spoke in a chilly tone. 'I don't think there's any need to make an issue of it, Nurse Lothian. I think we both know where we stand.' She stretched her lips into a thin condescending smile. 'For my part I'm willing to forget this unfortunate little contretemps.'

Vonne tried not to seethe. Sister was being magnanimous now, which was almost worse than enmity. But it must mean that she was not too sure of herself with the DN. That at least was gratifying.

Vonne said pleasantly, 'Mr Langham suggested I did a day shift for the time being.'

Sister Kent sat down again, but Vonne remained standing. After she had jotted a few notes on a pad, the Charge Sister said offhandedly, 'Yes, very well. Report tomorrow morning at seven.' She pointedly picked up the phone. 'If you'll excuse me . . .' It was a dismissal.

Vonne gladly escaped. She felt thoroughly shaken by the interview. Having someone take an instant dislike to her, which Sister Kent certainly seemed to have done, was a new and very unpleasant experience. It was worrying too, as Kirk seemed to be the key reason for it. And unless Sister Kent's attitude altered, she might be in for rather a rough time at Bauhinia Private Hospital. She really had been crazy to let Vicky persuade her into coming, Vonne thought yet again, as she made her way back along the corridors to the DN's office.

CHAPTER FOUR

WHEN Vonne arrived back at the house, Diana's car was in the driveway.

'Oh, good, you're back!' She hurried into the hall to greet Vonne before she was barely inside.

'Is anything wrong?' Vonne asked at once, surprised to see her since she had expected her to be at the pharmacy all day.

'No. I've got some news that might please you.'

'Oh?'

'You were saying last night that you wanted to buy a car as soon as possible—and I think I've found one for you.'

Vonne was of course keenly interested. She did not want to have to rely on Kirk, or Diana, for transport any longer than necessary. She knew Diana would object to her taking taxis, which was the only alternative as there was no public transport that would take her to and from the hospital.

'Tell me about it,' she urged, smiling.

'A friend of mine, Rina Robertson, dropped into the pharmacy today and asked if I knew anyone who'd like to buy a good-as-new red Honda hatchback.' Diana beamed triumphantly. 'Naturally I thought of you. Rina's recently had another baby, and needs something a bit bigger now she's got three youngsters,' she explained. 'So she's replaced the Honda. It's a nippy little car and I think you'll find it highly suitable.'

Vonne was delighted. 'When can I see it?'

'That's why I came home,' explained Diana. 'I phoned John to say I'd collect you, but you'd already left in a cab. Phyl's back today, so I left her in charge and dashed home straight away. I only beat you by a couple of minutes. We can go and look at the car straight away.'

'You must want to get back to the shop,' Vonne said. 'Couldn't I take a cab?'

Diana was adamant. 'Phyl can cope. I would have left it until this evening, but Rina's going out. I thought you'd be keen to see it right away.'

'I am—thank you,' Vonne said gratefully.

As they got into her car, Diana said, 'Rina's quite happy to take a down payment and the rest over three months or so. Will that suit you?'

'That would be marvellous!' Vonne was delighted. Most of the money she had was the proceeds from selling her car in England, and she was reluctant to lay out too much all at once if she could help it.

'Rina's a very pernickety person,' Diana said, expertly taking the bend at the end of the street which brought them on to a main road. 'So I think you can take it for granted that it's in good condition.'

Rina Robertson's house was a low-line contemporary style bungalow set in a tropical garden, rather wilder than Diana's, but attractive nonetheless.

'They had to rebuild after the cyclone,' Diana told Vonne. 'There wasn't a stick left standing.'

There were two cars in the driveway. One was the Honda. It was sparklingly clean and the paintwork looked to be in excellent condition. Rina heard their voices and came out to greet them. Tall and blonde, she had a warm smile and a ready handshake for Vonne.

'I hate to part with her really,' she said about the car, 'but I just had to get something a bit bigger. You can take her for a test drive if you like.' Without waiting for an answer, she suggested, 'But let's have a cuppa first. Can you stop too, Diana?'

Diana however declined. 'I'll let you two sort out the details between you. Rina will give you directions how to get home, Vonne.'

Diana departed and Rina led Vonne into the house. The baby was asleep, she said, and her other two children at school and kindergarten.

'Do you want to see the baby?' she asked, her eyes shining with the pride of recent motherhood.

'Of course!'

The baby was a tiny dark-haired girl—like her father, said Rina—with long lashes resting on petal-smooth cheeks.

'She's beautiful,' smiled Vonne, and it was ture. She remembered the tiny wrinkled new-born baby she had held so gingerly in her arms yesterday morning and the feeling of exultation it had given her to have helped it into the world.

'Yes, she is,' agreed Rina proudly. 'But I had a dreadful time having her—my worst pregnancy. If it hadn't been for Kirk, I doubt she'd be with us at all. He's a wonderful doctor—so dedicated.' She laughed, 'As you can see, I'm an ardent fan!'

As they stole out of the nursery, Rina said, 'You certainly got mixed up in a drama yesterday. Have you seen the story in the local paper?'

Vonne was embarrassed. 'No.'

'Hang on, I'll find it,' said Rina, marching to the kitchen with Vonne in her wake. 'It's a wonder you didn't have photographers and reporters bothering you. Kirk, I suppose, fobbed them off—he hates publicity of any kind. Now, where is it?' She opened a newspaper and thrust it at Vonne. 'There—look!'

While Rina brewed coffee, Vonne read the report. It was a short piece headlined 'Baby Born at Accident Scene'. Her part was described briefly—'The baby was safely delivered by an English nurse, Vonne Lothian, who had just arrived in this country. She is to take up a position at the Bauhinia Private Hospital shortly.' The report ended with the information that both mother and baby were doing well. She must go and see Nadia Laird as soon as she could, Vonne reminded herself.

Rina handed Vonne a cup of coffee. 'How does it feel to be famous on your first day?' she laughed.

'Embarrassing,' admitted Vonne wryly.

'You got to know Kirk when he was in England, I gather,' Rina remarked, obviously curious.

Vonne said, 'Yes, through a friend of my sister's.' It seemed that Rina knew nothing of Kirk's engagement to Vicky.

'All his friends feel it's time Kirk settled down,' Rina said seriously. 'He's much too nice to waste on bachelor-dom!' She chuckled and added warmly, 'I do hope you'll like Darwin, Vonne. It'll seem a bit strange at first, though, I suppose. It's rather different from what you must be used to.'

Vonne was dismayed at the assumption in her remarks. But she supposed it was only natural that those who knew nothing of Kirk's engagement should think there was something personal in her coming to Darwin.

She put Rina straight. 'You're jumping to conclusions, I'm afraid,' she said. 'There's nothing between Kirk and me.'

Rina pushed a plate of biscuits across the table. 'If you say so,' she said, but there was a twinkle in her eyes. 'But you are staying with his mother, so you can't blame people if they think—well . . .' She shrugged meaningfully.

'I'm only staying there because the units weren't finished in time,' said Vonne.

Rina remained unconvinced. 'Kirk's a mighty attractive man, though, wouldn't you say?' Her eyes challenged Vonne teasingly.

'He's good-looking,' Vonne conceded.

Rina pulled a face. 'I'd rather see him get hitched to someone like you than that bitch Lorin Kent.'

'I met her this morning,' Vonne mentioned, the unpleasant little scene still vividly in her mind.

'Did you?'

'I'll be nursing on her wards.'

Rina groaned. 'Poor you! Well, all I can say is watch out for her. She thinks she has first claim to Kirk's affections, and she won't take kindly to competition.'

'But I'm not competition!'

Rina said bluntly, 'Lorin is the jealous type. And she hasn't quite landed Kirk yet.' She glanced at the clock on the kitchen wall. 'Look—can you stay for lunch? I'd love to chat about England and London and all that. Joe and I were there a few years ago, before the kids came along, of course. I long to have a trip back.'

Vonne stayed and spent a pleasant couple of hours talking to Rina over lunch. While Rina fed the baby, Vonne washed up and then they discussed the car again. Rina refused any kind of formal contract.

'If Kirk thinks you're OK, that's good enough for me,' she insisted.

They left together eventually, Rina to pick up her children from school, and Vonne to find her way back to Diana's with the aid of a sketch map Rina had drawn for her. Driving back to Seaford Street, and reflecting on various remarks Rina had made, Vonne fell to wondering just how close Kirk and Lorin Kent had been before Vicky entered his life. Was it likely he would now fall into her arms again? The prospect of that happening gave her a sudden sharp desire to protect him. She laughed at herself. How crazy! Kirk could look after himself, and besides, it was none of her business.

At Diana's suggestion the evening was spent quietly since Vonne had to be up early in the morning.

'I do think you ought to have insisted on having a break first,' Diana chided.

But Vonne shook her head. 'I had a month in Barbados and a week back in England before I flew out. I'll be forgetting how to nurse if I don't get back to it soon.'

'You didn't forget yesterday,' Diana reminded her.

666

She tossed the local paper to Vonne. 'Look at this!'

Vonne said she'd already seen it. Diana was a trifle indignant about the story.

'They'd have splashed it a bit more, I'm sure, if Kirk had let them,' she said, 'but he probably told them you didn't want to be bothered. He thinks everyone else hates publicity the way he does.'

'Well, I do!' said Vonne fervently, and added, 'After all, I didn't do anything to make a fuss about. When a baby wants to be born, you don't have much option but to let it!'

Next morning she felt a little nervous as she set off for the hospital. Diana had drawn a map of the way for her, and she had also contacted Kirk to tell him that Vonne now had her own car.

Vonne wondered if she would see him today. She wondered too if he was aware yet that people were jumping to wrong conclusions about their relationship. If so he would probably avoid her like the plague.

She found her way to the hospital easily, swung into the car park and found a vacant space, being careful not to trespass on those spaces identified by registration numbers which she deduced were for doctors' cars.

Lorin was in her office. She greeted Vonne with chilly reserve, and a hint of yesterday's antagonism lingered in her eyes. It was a pity she had such cold eyes and a slightly discontented set to her mouth, Vonne thought, because she was a very attractive woman. But perhaps it was only to Vonne that she seemed lacking in warmth.

'Good morning!' She answered Vonne's greeting, briskly polite. 'You're just in time for briefing.' She managed to make it sound as though Vonne was late. 'We've got several new admissions this morning, and doctors will be popping in and out, I dare say.'

A nurse looked around the door. 'Oh—sorry. I didn't know you had anyone with you. I just wanted to ask if

Mrs Beatty is allowed to get up today?'

'Not until Dr Leveson has seen her,' advised Sister
Kent, and as the nurse turned to go, 'Just a minute,
Kelly. After briefing, would you take care of our new
nurse. Vonne Lothian had just arrived from England.
You can show her the ropes, see she has a uniform and so
on.'

'Oh—sure.' Kelly beamed at Vonne, her green eyes
lively with interest. 'Another pair of hands is just what
we need right now.'

Later, after the new shift had been briefed, Kelly took
Vonne under her wing. As she was showing her around,
she said wickedly, 'A word of friendly warning—watch
your step with Lorin. She's hard as nails and just as
sharp, but she runs her wards efficiently, I'll say that for
her. Nothing sloppy or slapdash about Lorin. By the
way, did she warn you to keep your hands off Dr
Leveson?'

'Not exactly . . .' Vonne was caught off guard.

Kelly hooted with laughter. 'So she did! Well, I
suppose you can't blame her. He's a prize worth fighting
for, and she's been working on it for a couple of years.
Lorin is desperate to get married, especially as she won't
enjoy being in her twenties for much longer. I wonder
how long he'll hold out. You have to admit she's a
stunning looker, and sexy with it!' She ran her eyes over
Vonne, who was now wearing the attractive pale blue
uniform with darker blue belt and matching collar
and cuffs. There was no cap. 'You make pretty fair
competition, though!'

'I hardly think so!'

They finished the tour of the wards and the various
other rooms attached such as the kitchen, pantry,
storeroom and sluice, then Kelly consulted the fob
watch pinned to her pocket.

'You can help me do the pre-meds for Dr Wang if you
like,' she offered.

Vonne worked with Kelly for most of the morning, assisting and learning the ropes. She met a couple of doctors who came in to see their patients, and she encountered several orderlies and theatre technicians. Dr Wang was a charming Chinese Australian with serene features and a gentle unhurried manner. Vonne could not imagine her ever becoming ruffled in the slightest.

She also met an anaesthetist, Bart Webb, when he came round to chat to patients due for operations later in the day. He was a tall, cheerful-looking man with dark wavy hair and smiling grey eyes that conveyed considerable interest and approval as he looked Vonne over.

'Nice to know you.' His voice had a gravelly drawl with a sensuous huskiness in it. 'I hope to get to know you better in due course.' He was suave, Vonne thought, and probably super-confident, but she liked him in spite of it. He had a very engaging manner which the patients obviously appreciated.

'I imagine that's very likely,' she responded, then realised that her answer might have sounded a little ambiguous. She blushed as she stumbled over words to rectify the blunder, and he laughed.

'Shall we make a start tomorrow night?' he suggested. 'Are you free for dinner?'

'B—but I've only just met you,' Vonne stammered.

'Around here you have to stake a claim before anyone else does!' he said confidentially. 'Where are you staying? I'll pick you up around seven-thirty, say.'

'I—I'm staying with Mrs Leveson in Seaford Street,' Vonne said, reluctantly, 'but really, I . . .'

His eyebrows rose and he seemed taken aback. 'Kirk's mother? I beg your pardon. I didn't realise I was trespassing.'

Vonne hastened to say, 'You're not—I mean, it's not—it's only that I met Kirk in England and he organised the job here for me—and—er—somewhere to stay until the nurses' quarters are finished.'

He was summing her up in a very thorough manner while she was speaking. 'So what you're saying is, Kirk's interest in you is purely avuncular?'

'Exactly.'

'He must be mad!' exclaimed Bart with a grin. 'But of course he does have other fish to fry. So there's no reason why you shouldn't come out with me tomorrow night?'

Vonne could hardly refuse now. And she was thinking that if it became known that she had accepted a date with Dr Webb, that would surely put paid to conjecture about her and Kirk. It might even make Lorin Kent more amenable towards her.

'None,' she said, smiling. 'Thank you. Seven-thirty will be fine.'

Vonne deliberately let slip to Kelly that she had made a date with Dr Webb, and was a little taken aback at Kelly's unexpected response.

Kelly slammed her fist into her other palm. 'I'm sorry, Vonne—I ought to have warned you. Bart Webb is the Don Juan of Bauhinia. He dates every new nurse on her first day. Nobody takes him too seriously, though. He's rather nice, but be careful. He might expect to be rewarded for his attentions, so you'd better make up your mind beforehand how far you're prepared to go.'

Vonne wished now that she hadn't accepted Bart Webb's invitation.

Kelly, however, was reassuring. 'Don't worry, you'll survive. Bart's not a boor. He does take no for an answer.' She laughed gaily. 'I guess he can afford to!'

In the middle of the afternoon, towards the end of her shift, Vonne received a message asking her to go along to the maternity ward. Lorin Kent delivered it with a look of displeasure. 'It's the woman whose baby was born in the car accident,' she said, adding, 'Don't be long.'

Vonne found Nadia in a ward on her own. She looked very different from the distressed girl who had suffered such anguish in the crashed car. The baby was in a cot beside her.

'Hello!' Vonne looked into the cot. The baby was awake and stared unseeingly up at her, tiny hands clutching the air.

'Isn't he wonderful?' exclaimed Nadia. 'Oh, I know all mothers think their babies are wonderful, but when I think . . .' she shuddered. 'Dr Leveson told me what happened—I can't really remember much about it myself. He said you were going to nurse here. Wasn't it lucky you were in the car with him?' She smiled shyly. 'I just wanted to thank you for what you did. I don't know how I would have borne it if my baby . . .' Tears filled her eyes.

Vonne squeezed her hand comfortingly. 'I didn't do much,' she said with a laugh. 'You did it all yourself!'

'But you were *there*,' said Nadia simply. 'You held my hand—I do remember that. I was so terrified!'

'Is your husband all right?' Vonne asked.

'Yes.' She brushed the tears away and laughed. 'It was so funny at first. He was in such a panic. I started having pains, you see, about three o'clock. I didn't expect the baby to come so soon and I thought I could easily last till morning, but all at once I realised things were happening faster than I'd expected. I'm afraid Adrian was in such a rush to get me to hospital he wasn't concentrating on his driving properly—and—well, you know the rest. Thank goodness the man in the other car wasn't badly hurt.'

Vonne chatted to her for a few minutes longer and then left. She was anxious not to incur Lorin's wrath. As she walked out of Nadia's room, she bumped straight into Kirk.

'Oh—sorry . . .' Her eyes met his and she saw the sudden painful flash of recognition. She had given him an unexpectedly sharp reminder of Vicky. His hands gripped her arms to steady her and she was a little shocked at the tremor that ran through her.

'Aren't you on Sister Kent's ward?' he asked, sounding annoyed at finding her off limits.

'Yes, I am, but Mrs Laird asked to see me for a few minutes.'

His mouth curved into a half smile. 'To thank you, of course.'

Vonne felt embarrassed. 'Yes, but as I told her . . .'

'No need to be too modest,' he said shortly, while his eyes drifted back and forth across her face, showing that he still found it difficult to believe she wasn't Vicky. It was the most disconcerting look she had ever experienced, a mixture of love and contempt, which although she knew it wasn't directed at her, hurt as though it was. As did his abrasive tone.

'I must get back,' she mumbled.

To her discomfort, he walked with her, not speaking, but exuding an almost palpable antipathy. They encountered Sister Kent just outside her office. She made her displeasure plain.

'You've been a long time, Nurse,' she said, as though Vonne had been deliberately gossiping.

'I'm sorry—I was only a few minutes . . .' Vonne bit her tongue, as she saw that the excuse was only going to earn her an even darker look.

'Go and help make up the beds in room three,' Lorin ordered peremptorily.

Vonne bridled at her tone, and wondered how long she would be able to put up with Lorin's only thinly veiled hostility. Sister Kent's long dark lashes fluttered provocatively at Kirk, and as Vonne walked away, she heard the girl's low, breathy voice inviting him into her office. She felt unaccountably prickly.

Just before she was due to finish her shift, Vonne was tidying up the ward kitchen when a figure appeared in the doorway. It was Kirk.

'I hear you've got yourself a car.' He leaned against the worktop she had been wiping down.

'Yes. Rina Robertson . . .' she began, but he interrupted.

'Mother told me about it.' His eyes followed her every move.

Vonne attempted to make small talk, but it wasn't very successful, especially as she felt so uncomfortable. She wished he would go. What had he come in for anyway? Unless it was to torture himself by looking at her because she was Vicky's twin. And then he'll snarl at me for not being her, Vonne thought bleakly.

But it wasn't Kirk who snarled. Sister Kent broke up the scene. Vonne was about to excuse herself when Lorin walked in. She glanced suspiciously from one to the other.

'So this is where you're lurking,' she rebuked Vonne caustically. 'Haven't you anything to do, Nurse?'

Vonne stifled a defensive retort and answered mildly, 'I was just tidying up the kitchen before I go off duty.'

Lorin glanced at her watch with a little snort, although she must have been well aware that the shift had ended, hers as well as Vonne's. 'Well, hurry up then. You're not expected to stand around wasting doctors' time.'

If Vonne expected a word of support from Kirk, she was disappointed. Maybe he would even enjoy seeing her rebuked. Any punishment, however trivial, would be deserved in his eyes, because of what Vicky had done to him.

Sister Kent said silkily, 'I thought you'd gone, Kirk —was there anything else you wanted?' Her voice was smoothly seductive.

Kirk flicked his eyes away from Vonne. 'Yes—I came back because I wanted to look at Mrs Hendry's case notes. Could you let me have them, please?'

'Of course, Doctor,' Lorin's tone was ingratiating. 'Right away.'

She swept out, and Kirk followed without a glance at Vonne. It was almost, Vonne thought with an unexpected pang, as though she had ceased to exist.

CHAPTER FIVE

VONNE felt exhausted mentally and physically by the time she reached Diana's house that afternoon. She made herself a cup of tea and stretched out on the lounger in the sun-room. Her feet ached, and her mind was in worse turmoil than ever. It had been quite a day, and she was glad to be alone for a while.

Her thoughts drifted eventually to Vicky and she wondered again, as she had wondered every day since they had parted, if all was well with her. Deep down she felt very anxious about her twin. She had not taken to Armand Saint-Germain on the only occasion she had met him, which of course didn't mean a thing. Vicky, she realised with a pang, had not really taken to Leith, and had voiced misgivings about their relationship in an oblique way. It was not really strange that even identical twins should be attracted to different kinds of men.

'I do hope she's happy,' Vonne murmured, worry creasing her brow. If only Vicky would hurry up and write! She had promised to, just as soon as she could, from Paris. Vonne reminded herself that she had only been in Australia three days, even though with so much having happened, it seemed longer.

She smiled to herself, picturing how her sister would chortle over the drama of that first day in Darwin. She was dying to write and tell her about it. Vicky would be anxious to hear about Kirk's reaction too, which would be more difficult to put into words.

She was idly watching a honey-eater darting from flower to flower outside the window when the stresses of the day caught up with her, and she drifted off. The phone startled her awake. She had only just scribbled down a message for Diana, when Kirk's mother came home. She looked as though she'd had as stressful a day as Vonne.

She slumped into a chair and kicked her shoes off. 'What a day! We were rushed off our feet, and we had a big consignment of supplies to unpack. I'm whacked!'

Vonne said, 'Put your feet up and I'll get your drink.'

'Oh, no, dear,' protested Diana, starting to rise. 'You've had a much more hectic day than I have, I'm quite sure.'

Vonne laughed. 'But I've had a sleep since I came home. I feel heaps better now. Go on, take it easy. I won't be around for ever!'

'I think I'd rather like a cup of nice strong tea, first,' said Diana with a hopeful look. And when Vonne had made it and brought it in to her she exclaimed, 'What an angel you are! I think I'll get sick and let you really spoil me!' She smiled affectionately. 'How nice it is to have you here, and what a relief to find you so easy to get along with. Now tell me, how did it go?'

Vonne spent another relaxing evening helping Diana to prepare a meal, and clear away afterwards, chatting as they worked together. Later, while the dishwasher gurgled away in the kitchen, they watched television and both retired early.

Diana seemed anxious when Vonne revealed that she was going out with Bart Webb the following night. She didn't exactly say she disapproved, but she came close to looking it.

'I don't know him very well,' she said, 'but gossip has it that fathers lock up their daughters—if they can —when he's around. He does have a rather devil-may-care charm, I grant you.' She added apologetically, 'Don't think for a minute I'm trying to interfere or tell you what you should or shouldn't do, but I think you might find more compatible partners than Bart Webb. I don't see you as his kind of woman.'

Vonne grimaced. 'From what I've heard, I don't think I am! But I can't get out of it now. I'll just have to risk my reputation.' Since Diana seemed so concerned, she decided to confess the real reason she had accepted his invitation. She finished by saying, 'So I thought if I went out with Bart, it would help to scotch any rumours about Kirk and me. You know what hospitals are like!'

Diana nodded. 'And small communities—everybody seems to know everybody else's business. Yes, I see what you mean.' Her smile was suddenly bright. 'If your sister is anything like you I can understand why Kirk fell head over heels in love with her. I wouldn't mind if the gossips did have something to gossip about.' Then she quickly added, 'I'm sorry, Vonne, that was a rather tactless thing to say, a purely selfish thought on my part.' She smiled wistfully. 'I was so looking forward to Kirk's getting married and my becoming a grandmother. My daughters both seem set on being career-women and not obliging me for some years yet.'

The next day Vonne felt depressed. Thoughts of Leith had invaded her dreams the previous night, but it had not been Angela who seemed to be coming between them. It had been Kirk who, every time she reached out to Leith, had dragged her away from him.

To her relief Vonne's second day at Bauhinia passed smoothly. Already the strangeness of a new workplace was wearing off and she was fitting comfortably into the routine. The other nurses were friendly and helpful, especially Kelly, who had a wonderfully optimistic view of life, as well as a wry humour which appealed to Vonne's own sense of the absurd, and inability to take some things too seriously.

Kelly was particularly adept at making fun of people without sounding unkind or sarcastic. Her chatter was spirit-lifting, and evidently the patients found it so too, because Vonne soon realised that the long-legged blonde was very popular with them.

The only jarring note in Vonne's day came from Lorin Kent. Several times the senior nurse found fault with what Vonne was doing or had done, but Vonne resisted any temptation to argue with her. She did not want to get involved in any unpleasantness.

Every bed under Lorin's charge was occupied, new patients coming in as others were discharged. They were all kept extremely busy.

'We have a pretty fast turnover of patients in this section,' Kelly told Vonne. 'Most of the D & Cs and tubal ligations and that sort of thing are admitted one day, gone the next, and you never get to know them. Mrs Beatty's been with us the longest at the moment. She's been in for two weeks, one of Dr Leveson's hysterectomies with minor complications.' She commented casually, 'I suppose you'll be seeing quite a bit of Kirk outside the hospital.'

'I don't expect so,' said Vonne.

'I just thought, with your living at his mother's place . . .'

Vonne shrugged. 'He got me the job, that's all. He doesn't live there, in any case.'

Kelly said, 'I let drop to Lorin that you were going out with Bart Webb. I thought it might get her off your back a bit.'

Vonne grinned. 'Thanks. But it hasn't! She's criticised just about everything I've done today. I'm beginning to think I need a refresher course.'

'Rubbish! She's just a nagger. I bet she was born carping about the inefficiency of the midwife! She's fed up with picking on the rest of us, so she's bound to work off her frustrations on a newcomer. It'll wear off after a bit.'

Vonne hoped she was right. She had worked under difficult conditions before, with irascible seniors and unreasonable doctors. It was all part and parcel of a nurse's job. Doctoring and nursing were tiring and

stressful jobs at the best of times and tempers often
became frayed, nerves fretted. Doctors and nurses had
to show enormous tolerance, ideally, but being human,
when stressed they often reacted in ways they didn't
intend to. Vonne had sometimes snapped at a junior
herself and later regretted it.

As she went off duty that afternoon, Kelly gave
Vonne a dig in the ribs and said wickedly, 'Enjoy your
date tonight. Don't do anything I wouldn't! Which gives
you plenty of scope!'

Vonne laughed. 'What are you doing tonight?'

Kelly pulled a face. 'Innocently washing my hair!'

Vonne was ready and waiting for Bart by seven-
fifteen. She felt nervous and wished she hadn't agreed to
go out with him so readily. It made her look too eager,
she thought regretfully, and he might have got the wrong
impression as a result.

She had chosen the demurest of her dresses, a burnt
orange shirtwaister with long sleeves and pleated skirt.
It looked very fetching with white accessories. At the
last minute she decided to wear her white shell necklace,
but when she looked for it, she couldn't find it.

'That's odd,' she muttered, sorting through the small
sandalwood box in which she kept her few pieces of
jewellery. She stopped and thought back to when she
had last worn it. Of course—that had been when Kirk
had driven her to the hospital for her interview with the
DN. She couldn't remember now taking it off afterwards. It had presumably fallen off in Kirk's car or at the
hospital.

'Blow,' she muttered, and fastened a gold chain
around her slender suntanned neck instead.

Diana had said she would be late home, probably after
Vonne had gone out, so when she heard the key in the
front door, Vonne was surprised. From where she was
sitting in the living-room, reading the newspaper, she
could see into the hall to the front door. She looked up,

waiting for Diana to appear. Instead, it was Kirk who let himself in.

'Oh!' Vonne was so taken aback she let out an involuntary exclamation. 'Hello, Kirk. I thought it was Diana home early after all. She said she'd be stocktaking until late tonight.' Suddenly she felt awkward, and totally confused by the intent way he was looking at her.

'Good evening, Vonne.' He strode into the room, his eyes showing involuntary masculine approval of the slim figure in the warm-toned dress. Vonne's heartbeat quickened. His way of looking at her was unnerving because she knew he was not seeing her, but Vicky. 'Going out?' he queried.

'Yes.'

His mouth quirked a little. 'A date?'

The way he said it made her inject a slight defensiveness into her reply. 'Yes.' She hoped he wouldn't probe.

'You don't waste any time, do you?' He was mildly sarcastic, and his eyes raked her in an oddly resentful way. 'May I know with whom—or is it a secret?'

'It's no secret. Bart Webb.'

'What?' His eyes blazed, and Vonne flinched at the force of his disapproval. 'You're going out with *him*?' He was scathing now.

'Yes—er—yes, I am.' He made her feel almost like a criminal. There was a disturbing glint in his eyes. The tawny depths smouldered with what she felt sure was jealousy. But of course it was only because she looked like Vicky. He was confused.

He said bitingly, 'Are you always bowled over so easily? You scarcely know the man.'

Vonne had to brave it out. 'Well, how do you get to know people if you don't go out with them?' she countered. It sounded lame.

To her astonishment, he grabbed her wrist and hauled her to her feet. He said, almost imploringly, 'For heaven's sake, Vonne, surely you can tell what he's like? Or do you like playing around?'

'Kirk! Let me go, please!' Vonne said tightly, trembling a little as the shock of his sudden touch ran through her.

He relaxed his hold but he did not let go. 'Do you?'

'Do I what?' She was alarmed by him now, yet in some strange way excited by his nearness.

'Like playing around?' He forced the words out through clenched teeth.

'No, of course not!'

'Then why are you so keen to go out with him?'

'Really, Kirk, I don't see that it's anything to do with you. I shall go out with whom I please. I don't know why you're making such a fuss.' She wanted to add, 'I'm not Vicky, so you've no reason to be jealous,' but that would have been cruel. As she looked into his face, seeing the anguish there, her heart went out to him and she desperately wanted to soothe and console, but dared not.

Abruptly Kirk let her go and stepped back a pace. 'No—neither do I!' He laughed sheepishly. 'Sorry!'

Vonne was relieved. 'It was kind of you to be concerned.'

He said nothing more for a moment or two, just raked her face with eyes that disconcerted but revealed nothing of his true feelings or thoughts. Then he shoved a hand in his pocket, saying, 'I nearly forgot—what I came round for was to return this. You dropped it in my car. The clasp had broken, so I fixed it for you.' He handed her the white shell necklace, dropping it into her outstretched hand, which trembled more than she wanted. She was touched that he had bothered to mend it for her.

'Oh, I'm so glad you found it,' she exclaimed. 'It's one of my souvenirs of Barbados and I didn't realise I'd lost it until I went to put it on tonight. Thank you so much for mending it, Kirk.' Their eyes met, and there was a look so near to tenderness in his that she looked quickly away, knowing it was not meant for her.

She was relieved when the doorbell rang. Without looking at Kirk, she snatched up her handbag and white cotton jacket, said good night and ran. She was not anxious for Bart and Kirk to meet. Kirk, she felt, was quite capable of embarrassing both her and Bart.

Bart stood smiling and eager on the porch, looking very debonair in a cream safari suit. Vonne forced herself to be cheery, but as she accompanied him to his car, her thoughts lingered in the house she had just left. Her rather dramatic effect on Kirk tonight, because she looked so much like her sister, worried her deeply. His seeing Vicky in her all the time would not help him to get over being jilted by her sister.

'I haven't had the pleasure of escorting such a ravishing redhead in years,' said Bart gallantly as Vonne settled into the passenger seat of his car. His hand strayed to her thigh and gave it a familiar pat. 'You're quite a stunner out of uniform, Vonne.'

She treated the remark facetiously. 'Oh, really? And there I was thinking the uniform became me rather well!'

He chuckled. 'Better than most!' His eyes twinkled with a goodnatured kind of lechery. 'I think you and I,' he said with conviction, 'are going to get along very well.'

'Where are we going?' Vonna asked brightly as the car eased away from the kerb.

'A snug little place I know where we can dine, and dance to smooth music.'

'Sounds great.' Bart's good humour made Vonne feel at ease again, even though she felt she might have to be wary of him later. But she would cross that bridge when she came to it.

The restaurant turned out to be an attractive small Italian place near the centre of town, with tables arranged on three sides of a small dance floor. On the fourth side was a stage where musicians were located. A board outside the restaurant listed the menu and promised a floor show later in the evening.

Bart slipped an arm around Vonne's waist as they entered. It was no more than a friendly guiding gesture, but she felt irrationally annoyed with him, as though he had taken a liberty.

It was obvious that he was a regular customer of Caravossi's. The waiter who greeted them knew him by name.

'A flower for the young lady?' the man offered, smiling appreciatively at Vonne. He selected an orchid from a basket on a side table and pinned it on her dress. No doubt it would be added to the bill, she thought.

'You are definitely an orchids lady,' said Bart, devouring her with eager eyes when the waiter had left them at their table while he went to fetch the menu and the wine list Bart had requested.

'Hardly,' Vonne replied. 'I don't have the sort of friends who can afford to buy me orchids.'

Bart laughed. 'Not in England, perhaps. But these grow wild here. Darwin is a natural hothouse!' He added, as the waiter returned, 'Something to drink while we make up our minds about food?'

'Dry vermouth and tonic, please,' said Vonne, and made a mental note to be careful not to drink too much wine.

In the lull after they had ordered, Bart said, 'Would you like to dance?' The band was playing a slow dreamy number and several couples were moving moodily across the floor.

'Not yet,' she said, 'that is, if you don't mind. I've been on my feet all day,' she reminded him.

He nodded smilingly, 'I can't say I wouldn't like to hold you in my arms right away,' he said candidly, 'but I can wait. Meanwhile I shall gaze into your beautiful velvety brown eyes and listen to you telling me all about yourself.'

'Are you always so corny, Bart?' Vonne laughed teasingly. 'Do you flatter all your girl-friends with orchids and extravagant compliments?'

He pretended to be hurt. 'My dear girl, anyone would think . . .'

Vonne chimed in lightly, 'Well, from what I've heard at the hospital . . .'

He exclaimed in mock outrage, 'All right—tell me who's been talking? Whatever they said it's all lies. I'm not guilty. Must have been some other fellow they were talking about.' A more sober expression chased the fun from his eyes. He reached across the table and captured her fingers which were idly toying with a salt cellar. 'Vonne, I guess it's true I have a bit of a reputation —what bachelor hasn't?—but I think I can honestly say I only behave the way people expect or want me to. I hope you don't believe all you hear.'

He looked so innocent, Vonne was amused. It would be impossible, she realised, to dislike or be angry with Bart Webb. And that could make things difficult.

'I form my own judgments of people,' she said.

His look was admiring. 'You're not just a pretty face, are you, Vonne?'

She shrugged. 'I hope not! Are you?'

His infectious laughter caused a couple at a nearby table to glance across at them and smile.

'Come on, let's dance,' urged Bart impulsively. 'You can pickle your feet in Radox when you get home. The first course always takes ages to come because they expect the customers to dance.'

Vonne did not want to spoil the evening by being difficult, so she got up with him. As she expected, he held her close, resting his cheek against her temple and giving her little room to avoid it. The music was romantic, but Vonne felt no response within her at Bart's closeness. And yet, when she thought of Leith, with whom she had never danced, there was a similar blank feeling accompanying the thought, not the intensely painful longing she had expected. Perhaps she was getting over him at last.

After a few minutes, Bart said, 'What's the matter, Vonne? You're as tense as a surgeon doing his first op! Relax, girl, relax—Uncle Bart won't bite.' And he nibbled her ear and chuckled seductively into it.

Vonne hadn't realised she was so rigid. She laughed and tried to relax in his arms.

'That's better,' he approved. 'Now you feel more like a real woman than a plaster cast!'

'I think our meal has arrived,' said Vonne, catching a glimpse of a waiter approaching their table.

Over the meal, Bart asked her innumerable questions about herself. Vonne told him what she had told everyone else—only part of the truth. She did not mention Kirk's and Vicky's engagement, but she did tell him that her sister was marrying a Frenchman. 'At least,' she thought, 'I hope she is.' Her worries over Vicky resurfaced and she wished again that a letter would come soon. She couldn't write to Vicky until she knew her address in Paris.

Bart asked a few questions probing in a roundabout way her relationship with Kirk, evidently not entirely satisfied with what she had said before. Vonne could only repeat it, with supporting details.

'I bet Lorin feels uneasy, you living in his mother's house,' commented Bart. 'She regards Kirk as her territory.'

'Perhaps he is,' Vonne said innocently.

'She wants to get married,' said Bart, with faint distaste, 'but Kirk won't take the bait until he's ready for it, and she's starry-eyed enough to play it his way, I reckon. There's plenty would say he's lucky, I suppose.'

'Including you?'

He smirked ingratiatingly, and his voice dropped to a seductive purr. 'Not now I've met you, sweetheart.'

Vonne quickly diverted the conversation in another direction. 'You've heard all about me,' she said, 'so what about telling me about you?'

His face suddenly closed up at the question. 'Not much to tell, Vonne. I'm just a typical runaway.'

'What do you mean?'

Bitterness twisted his mouth. 'You'll come across a lot of fellows up here running away from something—wives, de facto wives, debts, indiscretions, tax . . .'

'What was your crime?'

For a moment she thought he wasn't going to answer, but finally he said, 'I'm not really a bachelor. I have a wife in Sydney. She walked out on me and took up with this other guy—a medico mate of mine, thank you very much—then told the judge I had a—er—drink problem —and she got custody of the girls . . .' Suddenly his voice broke emotionally. 'Heck, why am I telling you this? I've never told anyone round here before.'

Vonne attempted a word of sympathy, but he brushed it all aside. 'I don't deserve any sympathy, Vonne. I was a louse, and I guess she had good reasons for walking out—but the little girls, I couldn't stand losing them, just seeing them odd weekends. It was better not at all. I just had to run.' There was a long pause while he stared mournfully into his wineglass, then he swiftly downed the contents and grinned at her as he refilled it, and hers. 'Cheers, Vonne! Eat, drink and be merry, for tomorrow we return to the bondage of Bauhinia! Be a pal and forget everything I just said, will you?'

'Of course, Bart.'

'Let's dance again,' he said, standing up eagerly.

Vonne felt sorry for him. That brash, happy-go-lucky exterior hid a private tragedy that apparently few, if anyone, suspected. Maybe it explained why he had the reputation of being a Don Juan. People did sometimes hide their unhappiness under wild behaviour.

They left the restaurant before the floor show came on. Vonne had pleaded tiredness. 'I won't be able to get up in the morning if I don't get some sleep.'

Bart was agreeable. 'Whatever you say, sweetie. We'll come again when there's no work tomorrow.'

Vonne felt very sleepy when she got into the car, and it was some minutes after they had left the restaurant that she began to feel instinctively that they were not on the way to Seaford Street.

'Bart, where are we?' she asked cautiously.

'Just taking a run up to East Point to see the moonrise,' he said, 'Nearly there.'

Vonne tensed. 'Bart, I don't think . . .'

'Here we are!' He turned the car abruptly and braked. Ahead of them Vonne could dimly see a line of pandanus palms and beyond that a dark ocean, with a silvery trail across it from the moon riding high in a star-littered sky.

'Bart, the moon's already up,' she said, her voice unsteady.

'So it is! Well, never mind.' He turned and pulled her into his arms. 'So, who needs a moon?' he murmured as he matched his lips hungrily to hers.

Vonne tried not to panic. It was important to keep cool and not get angry if she could avoid it. I have to work with him, she reminded herself.

For a moment or two she allowed him to kiss her but showed no response whatsoever, hoping this would deter him. When he tried to arouse her by increasing his ardour, she resisted, pushing him away firmly.

'Please, Bart—I wouldn't have come out with you if I'd thought . . .'

She could just make out the petulance in his expression. 'You said you knew all about my reputation, but you still came . . .'

'I said I make my own judgments. And you said you never do anything that isn't welcome.'

He was smiling as his hand strayed under the neckline of her dress and his warm fingers caressed the cool skin, moving downwards to her breast, testing her. Vonne firmly but gently removed it. 'No, Bart, I mean it.'

He looked directly into her eyes. 'I believe you do.' He backed off slightly but still held her. 'I guess I never learnt much about women. Forgive?'

She could only say, 'What for? You haven't done anything.'

He laughed. 'Vonne, you're a little witch—and I've a feeling you're going to drive me wild!'

'You can drive me home, please,' she said with asperity. 'Right now! I've got to be up at six.' But she smiled as she said it.

To her relief he didn't try to make an issue of it. He merely leaned over and kissed her lightly on the lips, saying, 'Will you come out with me again if I promise to behave?'

'If my company is all you want, yes,' she said. Bart didn't answer.

He drove back much too fast for Vonne's comfort, but she did not dare ask him to slow down. She was relieved when they turned into Diana's street, and Bart pulled up outside the house.

Vonne thanked him. 'It was a very enjoyable evening,' she said.

'Thank *you*, Vonne. Sorry I went too fast.' She knew he wasn't only referring to his driving.

Vonne got out quickly lest he should read into any hesitation on her part, a desire to be detained. 'Good night,' she said, closing the door.

'Sweet dreams,' he replied, as the car slid away from the kerb.

Vonne ran down the driveway, not sure why she ran, since she wasn't afraid of anything. She almost tripped in the darkness and was flung forward, uttering a little cry as she fell. But instead of sprawling on the concrete, she was caught and held hard against a rock-solid body. Strong arms encircled her tightly, knocking all the breath out of her.

'Vonne! What's up?' The deep timbre of his voice sent a shockwave through her that was nothing to do with surprise.

'Oh—Kirk! You gave me a fright,' she managed to gulp. She attempted to step away from him, but he held her fast. His face was so close she could see his expression clearly in the moonlight that filtered through the foliage above them. She was alarmed at the expression the pearly light revealed in his eyes.

'What were you running away from? Bart?' He sounded angry.

She shook her head vigorously. 'No! Of course not. I was just—running. I don't know why. I just felt like it, I suppose.' She felt foolish not having a logical explanation. It made his assumption seem all the more likely.

His hold on her relaxed. It was the moment to say good night and continue on into the house, but she didn't move—no, couldn't move. She must be tipsy, she thought in a strange lightheaded way. Too much wine, perhaps . . .

And that, surely, was the only reason, she reflected later, that she let him kiss her. It happened suddenly, a swift pounce that jerked her hard against him again, with one arm tightly encircling her waist and his hand spread across the small of her back. His fingers were powerful and warm through the thin material of her dress, as they gently but persuasively massaged her spine. His other hand lightly cupped her face so that she could not, even if she had wanted to, prevent his lips from moving on hers with a deeply passionate rhythm. Her own parted involuntarily, unable to resist the call of her own desires, to allow a deeper and more passionate embrace, and the shockwaves coursing through her were as unexpected as they were extraordinary.

It was uncannily like that moment months ago when he had kissed her by mistake in Sylvia's garden in London. She was responding now with the same impulsiveness as she had then. But this time she knew whom she was kissing, and this time it was she who came to her senses first and pulled back, thoroughly agitated.

'Kirk . . .' Her lips trembled from his touch, and she was shaking uncontrollably inside, although outwardly quite calm.

He seemed to be hypnotised. With a strange little smile curving his mouth he ran his fingers lightly up through her curls, caressing the nape of her neck with exquisite tenderness. 'Why in heaven's name do you have to look so much like Vicky?' he muttered in a desperate entreaty.

'I—I'm sorry . . .' Vonne whispered.

He released her abruptly. 'No—I should be.' There was still an underlying anger in his voice. 'Good night, Vonne.'

'Good night, Kirk,' she whispered, and fled.

CHAPTER SIX

THE next day there was a letter from Vicky, sent care of the hospital. There wasn't much news in it; Vicky was a hopeless letter-writer. Her large, rather childish and almost illegible scrawl slanted across the blue airletter form with the Paris postmark in widely spaced lines.

All it really said was that she was fabulously happy, that Armand was wonderful, and that she was working in a French clinic with him. His family were fantastic and his friends fascinating. She hoped Vonne had had a good trip and that everything was working out all right. She begged Vonne to write and tell her all about it soon, and ended with profuse apologies, and thanks for everything.

Vicky avoided actually mentioning Kirk's name, but Vonne knew she must be dying to know how he had taken the news. She wasn't sure what she would say about that to her sister. The address on Vicky's letter was an apartment in Paris. Vonne wondered if she was living there alone, or with Armand. There was no mention of marriage. Although Vicky's letter was breezy and full of her new-found happiness, it did not drive away Vonne's anxiety. Was the letter perhaps too bright, too breezy, too full of superlatives?

Don't be silly! she mocked herself. You're imagining things. She's on top of the world.

At lunchtime Bart Webb joined Vonne at her table in the canteen. She was sitting alone for once. As he sat down, Vonne noticed a group of nurses she knew slightly, at another table, glancing in her direction and then whispering to each other. She decided she didn't care if they gossiped about her and Bart, so long as they didn't gossip about her and Kirk.

'Hello, Vonne.' Bart seemed rather subdued. There were dark shadows under his eyes as though he hadn't slept.

'Hello, Bart.' She purposely injected an extra cheery note into her voice so he wouldn't think she was annoyed with him over last night.

Nevertheless he was still anxious. 'Not still mad at me, are you?'

Vonne smiled. 'Mad at you? Of course not!'

'I spoilt your evening, didn't I, behaving like a boor?' It seemed to be weighing heavily on him.

Vonne could have told him that it hadn't been he who had spoiled the evening, but Kirk. What she did say was, 'Perhaps you think I spoiled yours? I had a lovely time, Bart. Thank you again.'

He still seemed unconvinced. 'I don't want you to have the wrong idea about me, Vonne. I'd very much like to take you out again, and I promise—on your terms.' A ghost of a smile crinkled his mouth.

Vonne tensed. 'Can you keep promises?'

He pretended outrage. 'Try me!'

'All right, I will.' She had made up her mind last night that she wouldn't risk going out with him again, but today his obvious sincerity made it hard to refuse.

He suggested eagerly, 'What about your next day off?'

'I'm off Friday and Saturday next week.'

'We'll go sightseeing,' Bart decided. 'You haven't seen much of Darwin yet, I suppose?'

'No, I haven't, but Mrs Leveson has promised to show me round.'

He looked thoughtful. 'Do you swim?'

'Yes.'

'Good. We'll go to Berry Springs. It'll give you a chance to see something of the bush, and we can take a picnic lunch. How does that grab you?'

'Great. I'll bring the lunch.'

'Shall we make it Friday? It'll be less crowded then.'

Vonne narrowed her eyes suspiciously and he laughed. 'No ulterior motive, I assure you. I just don't care for swimming with crowds. But if you'd prefer Saturday . . .'

'Friday will be fine,' said Vonne. She pushed her chair back. 'I must be going.'

Bart had almost finished his lunch. He clashed his knife and fork together and gulped down his tea, anxious to leave with her. Vonne was aware of the other nurses staring. It was bound to be all over the hospital that Bart Webb was flirting with the new nurse from England.

As they were walking along the corridor from the canteen, Kirk appeared. Vonne recoiled at the look he gave her, but Bart did not seem to notice the disapproval in the gynaecologist's eyes.

'Ah, Kirk—I wanted a word with you . . .' he said.

Vonne slipped away and hurried back to her wards. Lorin Kent greeted her with a sharp admonitory look that suggested she had overrun her lunch hour, even though she hadn't.

Lorin said, 'Mrs Tyboe is having her op today. You can do her pre-med and you can also special her after the op for a couple of days.' She added with a slight sniff, 'You seemed to be enjoying yourself last night at Caravossi's.' Her frosty blue eyes were sharply curious.

Vonne had not noticed Lorin at the restaurant. She wondered whom she'd been with. Not Kirk, certainly, because Diana had said he'd been with her all evening.

'I had a very pleasant time,' Vonne said.

'It didn't take you long to find yourself an escort,' Lorin observed, a little acidly, echoing Kirk's remark.

It was the sort of comment to which there was really no appropriate answer, so Vonne gave none. She thought she detected relief in the senior nurse's eyes and was glad Lorin had seen her out with Bart. It did not, however, soften Lorin's attitude towards her.

Sister Kent, even though her fears must have surely been somewhat allayed, remained coolly aloof and critical of Vonne. During the next few days Vonne's patience was sorely tried. There were times when she felt that everything that went wrong on the wards was her fault alone. A week seemed more like a month, and if it hadn't been for the fact that Vonne loved nursing she might well have hated every minute at Bauhinia in those first days.

'I'm beginning to think I'm not competent,' she complained to Kelly after one particularly caustic comment from Lorin. 'I can't seem to do anything right for her!' Or for Dr Leveson, she could have added. Kirk seemed to be becoming daily more abrasive with her.

'Of course you're competent,' soothed Kelly. 'Lorin's always like this with newcomers. It makes her feel super-efficient always to be finding fault with others.'

'But I have made some mistakes . . .' Vonne said gravely. 'Nothing too serious, it's true, but she puts me off my stroke.' So did Kirk, only she didn't say so.

Fortunately, as well as her fellow nurses, there was Bart to keep her spirits up. He always had a quick quip to make her laugh, and if she didn't altogether welcome the way he slipped his arm around her waist and the way his eyes seemed to peel her clothing off, she didn't let it bother her too much. Kirk bothered her much more, in a very different and more disturbing way.

Whenever he came to see patients, she tried to keep well away, but this was not always possible. He perpetually crossed her path, and always with that lingering look that was half angry accusation, half a kind of futile longing. It made her feel guilty just for being there. His attitude made her nervous and her normally calm concentration on what she was doing was always disturbed when he was around.

'He seems to spend a lot of time here,' she remarked to Kelly, one morning while they were having a quick cup of coffee during a break, and after Kirk had caught her by surprise again.

Kelly nodded. 'He was always in and out a lot, but I think you're right, he does seem to be here more often lately, on some pretext or other. Maybe it's because of Lorin. She lets him do as he likes, of course. No one else would dare riffle through her files looking at patients' notes the way he does. Dr Leveson can do no wrong as far as she's concerned.'

The next morning Kirk again arrived unexpectedly in one of the wards where Vonne was attending to a patient. She glanced across at him, and he said, 'I'm just going to have a word with Mrs Duke, Nurse.' He waved a slim folder at her. 'I fished out her notes myself.'

The patient Vonne was attending to whispered, 'Dr Leveson's wonderful, isn't he?'

Vonne nodded absently. Her skin was prickling just because he was in the room.

'I wouldn't go to anyone else.' The young woman's smile was not far short of adoring.

'I believe he's an excellent gynaecologist,' Vonne agreed, determined not to get into any discussion of Dr Leveson's personal characteristics, at least not while he was within earshot! She had very quickly become aware that he was not only professionally admired, but also very popular. Patients tidied their hair and straightened their covers when it was known he was about to visit.

As Vonne was leaving her patient, Kirk swept through the curtains surrounding the bed across the room and she almost collided with him. She shrank from his gaze. He looked considerably annoyed, and she began to feel guilty automatically, without even knowing what was wrong. He waved a form in her face.

'What use is this when half the information isn't there?' he demanded in a fierce undertone.

'I—I beg your pardon?'

'This!' He stabbed the paper. 'Whoever filled this in

obviously didn't ask the patient half the questions.' He thrust it at her. 'Was it you?'

As Vonne tried to take the form, her fingers brushed his and she managed to fumble and drop it. It fluttered to the floor and in the breeze created by Kirk's turning round, blew under the curtains around the bed next to them. Vonne was obliged to scramble after it, only to find that the paper had slightered right under the bed. She was retrieving it in a very undignified fashion when Lorin marched in.

'Nurse Lothian! What on earth are you doing?'

Now every patient in the ward was agog.

Red-faced and embarrassed, Vonne stood up with the form in her hand.

Kirk said in a low, scathing tone. 'Nurse Lothian seems to be a bit of a butterfingers.'

Vonne felt humiliated, especially as all the patients in the five-bed ward could probably hear. But even worse was to come.

Kirk turned grimly to Lorin. 'There are some serious omissions on this.' He snatched the piece of paper from Vonne's quivering fingers and thrust it at Lorin, darting an accusing look at Vonne as he did so. 'The patient has had two previous operations and she's allergic to penicillin. I don't see how anyone who wasn't thoroughly careless could fail to establish that!' He added, 'Just as well I know my own patients.'

Lorin ran her eyes down the form. She looked up fluttering her lashes provocatively at Kirk, and said in what purported to be a placatory tone, 'I'm sorry. Vonne is still rather new here, and sometimes she does seem to have other things on her mind. I assure you it won't happen again.'

Vonne nearly exploded with indignation, but she managed to keep cool as she answered in a tight little voice, deliberately kept low enough so that the patients could not hear, 'I did not fill in Mrs Duke's form.'

She could see that Kirk was reluctant to believe her.

Lorin's face was disdainful, and there was a triumphant glitter in her eyes. She did not back Vonne up. She merely said, 'If you've finished in here, Nurse, you can strip the beds in number four. We have three new admissions this afternoon.'

Vonne went with as much dignity as she could muster. She was livid with Lorin for not supporting her, and she felt sure she knew why. It was the most monstrous thing Lorin had done so far.

Later in the day she managed to check with Mrs Duke, who was slightly deaf and had not heard the conversation that morning, and she discovered it had been, as she suspected, Lorin herself who had completed—or rather not completed—the form. It wouldn't have been carelessness—Lorin was never careless. It was more likely she had been interrupted. What made Vonne fume was that she had managed to lay the blame on her while appearing tolerant. There was nothing she could do about it. It would only antagonise Lorin all the more if she complained.

Outside the hospital, Vonne did not see Kirk for some days. When Diana remarked once, 'You and Kirk always seem to be missing each other,' and gave her a rather speculative look, Vonne decided he was probably doing his best to avoid her. Sometimes she longed to ask Diana if Kirk had confided in her at all over Vicky, but she felt that would be presumptuous, so she said nothing, hoping that Diana might mention it herself. However, she did not, and Vonne guessed that Kirk's passion for privacy kept even his mother in ignorance.

Diana insisted on keeping her promise to show Vonne around the city and some of the more interesting sights nearby, so on a couple of evenings she got away early and took Vonne for a drive. One evening they went up to East Point to see the old World War Two artillery emplacements and the sunset. Although she wasn't absolutely sure, Vonne guessed that this was where Bart had brought her on the pretext of seeing the moon rise. She did not, however, tell Diana she had been there before.

When Friday came and Vonne knew she had two full days off, she woke with a great sense of relief. It would be nice to be free of the carping Lorin Kent for forty-eight hours, and the even worse tension of never knowing when she might encounter Kirk. The thought of a day out with Bart was a pleasing prospect and she felt sure he would keep his promise.

She was aware that Diana did not approve of her developing a relationship with Bart. Diana did not actually say so, but her manner suggested she was less than enthusiastic.

Vonne wore a bikini under her jeans and short caftan-style top, and made sure she was equipped with hat, sunglasses and tanning lotion. She had packed their lunch in a polystyrene cool-box that Diana had lent her, the night before, and was ready and waiting when Bart arrived.

He looked very casual in shorts and a T-shirt, and a floppy white cotton hat, with sandals on his feet. Vonne remembered suddenly what he had told her on their first date about his wife and children. Bart concealed his private tragedy well, she thought, with a pang of sympathy.

'All set?' He carried the lunch box out to the car and Vonne followed with her denim carryall.

'Do you like birds?' asked Bart as they roared off down the street.

Vonne couldn't resist teasing. 'Not as much as you do, I'm sure!'

He laughed, 'I'm interested in the feathered variety as well as the curvy, cuddly kind!' He shot her a mocking look and she contrived to look suitably prim in response.

He went on, 'We ought to see a lot of birds at Berry Springs. There are always rainbow bee-eaters there, and we should see several different kinds of parrots. I've brought binoculars, so you can learn something at first hand about our wildlife.'

'I'm dying to see kangaroos,' confessed Vonne.

'You might be lucky,' said Bart, 'but they're most easily seen at dawn and dusk. If we don't spot any, we'll go to Yarrawonga on the way back. There's a good selection of birds and animals at the sanctuary. Have you ever seen a croc?'

'Crocodiles?'

'Yep. Rivers are full of 'em up in this part of the world. You have to watch your step.'

Despite his straight face, Vonne suspected he was teasing her, but she said cautiously, 'There aren't any at Berry Springs, I hope.'

'We-ell, I can't say I've ever been attacked by one there, but . . .' He glanced aside and laughed at her because she still wasn't sure whether to be anxious or not. 'Don't worry, it's only the salties that are dangerous. The freshwater crocs are harmless. It's the green tree ants you need to be careful of. Cop a couple of them down the back of your shirt—or front—and you'll really know about it!'

Vonne began to have grave misgivings about the attractions of the Australian bush. 'Are there any other dangerous animals and insects?' she asked nervously.

'Not really. You mind your business, they'll mostly mind theirs. Seriously, though, you need to watch out for snakes and scorpions, and there are one or two spiders that are poisonous, but as likely as not you'll never come across any of them. I come from Sydney, which is notorious for the funnel-web spider. It can be a killer, but in all my life there I never even saw one! Of course, the big lizards usually scare the wits out of the tourists, but they're harmless. You'd be wise to shin up a tree if you're charged by a water buffalo—but they're not native . . .'

'Stop!' begged Vonne. 'It sounds terrifying!'

He laughed and patted her knee. 'You've nothing to worry about, Vonne. You're with me!'

His hand caressed her thigh and he shot her a rather torrid glance. Vonne wondered if she had been wise to trust him after all. Maybe Bart Webb was the only dangerous creature in the bush so far as she was concerned. The car slewed dangerously and she removed his hand and placed it firmly back on the steering wheel.

'Keep your mind on the road, Bart,' she advised.

After that, he did, and kept up a flow of interesting information on the passing scene. He pointed out the curious bottle-shaped baobab trees, and told her how the giant termite hills that dotted the landscape like tombstones were angled so as to minimise the effect of the hot sun on their inhabitants.

Vonne laughed at a sign that said 'We like our lizards frilled, not grilled! No bushfires!' over a picture of a quaint frilled lizard. She recognised the seriousness of it too; there was a good deal of blackened bush along their route.

There were only a few people at the picnic spot. Bart led her a short distance from the main group to a more secluded spot where trees overhung the sparkling spring water.

'How about this?' he suggested, looking to her for approval.

'Perfect,' agreed Vonne. 'Just the place to relax. It's so lovely and peaceful here.'

He laid an arm across her shoulders. 'I guess you deserve it. You've had a tough week?'

'It has been rather hectic,' she conceded, moving away from him as naturally as she could.

'You're not regretting you came to Darwin, I hope.'

'No, not at all.' That was a lie. Every day she wished

she had not let Vicky talk her into coming. Even as she spoke, Kirk's tormented face flashed into her mind. She had made it much worse for him, and she regretted that, but it was he, after all, who had insisted she honour her contract.

Suddenly Bart said, in a hushed tone, 'Look, over there—rainbow bee-eaters!'

Vonne followed his pointing finger and glimpsed a flash of brilliant colour. Bart dragged the binoculars from his bag and they spent half an hour absorbed in watching the colourful small birds wheeling and diving from a vine strung across the water, as they fed on bees and other insects.

There were other birds there too. A grey thrush that poured forth a powerful melody, and competed with the echoing bell notes of the pied butcher-bird. Rainbow lorikeets and other parrots skimmed through the trees over their heads, screeching and whistling as they fed on nectar in the gum blossom, and seeds.

Bart suggested a swim before lunch. 'The water is always pleasantly warm,' he told Vonne. 'Very relaxing.'

Presently, when they unpacked their lunch, they were visited by more birds. The butcher-birds became very bold and hung around for titbits. A blue-winged kookaburra perched on a branch so close that Vonne did not need the binoculars to see his beady brown eye quite clearly.

'They're not the same as the southern species,' Bart told her. 'That's the one you see in all the pictures. This fellow has different colouring.'

They lazed on the bank for an hour or so, then he reminded her that if they were to visit Yarrawonga, they must start back soon. His eyes drifted over her bikini-clad body as though he would rather linger, but he made no advances to her.

At Yarrawonga, Vonne saw her first kangaroos. One

came up to her to see if she had anything to give it to eat. She stroked its soft inquisitive nose and tickled it behind the ears, wondering, as she looked into the trusting brown eyes, how anyone could possibly kill or be cruel to such a beautiful creature.

The crocodiles filled her with an instinctive revulsion at first. Their fearsome jaws almost seemed to be smiling, but whether with mirth or relish for a recent or anticipated meal, she couldn't decide. She was glad they were safely fenced in.

Bart was indulgently amused by her delight in everything she saw, and kept a companionable arm around her waist as they walked around the park. Back in Darwin he dropped her off at Diana's house, promising to pick her up later to go out for a meal.

'I'm in the kitchen,' Diana called out as Vonne came in. She exclaimed, 'Well, you look as though you've had a splendid day!'

'I have!' said Vonne with enthusiasm. She started to empty the lunch-box. 'What a delicious place Berry Springs is. So very relaxing.'

As she spoke she was suddenly skin-tinglingly aware of a presence behind her and turned. Kirk was standing in the sun-room doorway observing her with a slightly sardonic gaze.

'Perhaps it was the company that helped you to relax,' he remarked, and his eyes devoured her with the look she knew so well and which thoroughly disconcerted her.

She knew Diana would have told him she was out with Bart. She wanted to say, 'It's no use your being jealous of Bart—I'm not Vicky!' but she dared not.

'Are you in for dinner?' Diana wanted to know.

'No. At least, if it's all right with you, Bart's calling for me later,' Vonne told her.

Diana made coffee and Vonne was persuaded to join them before she went to change for the evening. They sat in the sun-room talking, and Vonne was grateful that Diana was there. She felt more uncomfortable now with Kirk than on the first day. His antagonism towards her seemed to be growing rather than abating. She understood what he must be feeling, but that didn't make it any easier for her.

After a few minutes, Diana left them to attend to the cooking. Vonne wondered if Kirk was staying for dinner.

Kirk suddenly said into the silence that had followed his mother's departure, 'Have you heard from Vicky?'

'Yes, I have.' Vonne felt she had to explain, so she said with a laugh, 'She's an infuriating letter-writer! She just said she was all right.'

Not a muscle in his face moved to betray his feelings.

'Would you like her address?' Vonne asked tentatively, not sure whether it was the right thing to do or not.

Kirk shook his head decisively. 'No, I don't think I have anything to say to Vicky. Least said soonest mended, eh?'

'I suppose so,' Vonne agreed, dragging her eyes away from his, because she was suddenly reminded with alarming vividness of the night he had kissed her after she had been out with Bart. The memory sent a sudden flash of fire through her limbs that both startled and embarrassed her, as though it would have been visible to him.

'I'd better go and change,' she said, hastily getting up.

He rose too. 'And I must be going.' A glimmer of a smile. 'I have a date tonight too.'

'Oh?' It wasn't that she was surprised, only taken aback that he should have mentioned it at all.

'Yes, I'm taking Lorin to a film,' he said casually, and his eyes met hers with a look that was almost defiant.

For heaven's sake, she thought, he expects me to be jealous! Or rather Vicky.

'I hope you enjoy it,' she said, but as she hurried off to her room she felt an irrational dismay. She didn't want Kirk to be caught on the rebound by Lorin Kent.

He was gone when she reappeared.

'That's pretty,' complimented Diana on the pale green Liberty print with demure white collar and cuffs that Vonne was wearing.

'Half price at a sale!' revealed Vonne.

Diana chuckled. 'You're like me, I expect. I adore sales. The trouble is I too often buy things I don't need.'

If the evening was any less enjoyable than the day, it was not Bart's fault, Vonne reflected once or twice. He was attentive but not pushy, and he never once let the conversation flag. But somehow she kept letting her attention wander from what he was saying to worry about Kirk and his odd behaviour. It really did seem sometimes as though he was deluding himself that she actually was her sister.

But more than that she worried about Kirk and Lorin Kent. He might marry Lorin just to spite Vicky, and later regret it. But what could she do about it? Vonne thought. It was no business of hers, anyway, what Kirk did.

During the next few weeks Vonne frequently went out with Bart Webb. She had tried not to let it develop into a steady arrangement, but it was always hard to say no when she didn't have a plausible excuse, and besides, he always behaved impeccably. There were some, she often thought wryly, Kirk included, who probably wouldn't have believed that.

It was a bit hard to believe it herself sometimes, knowing his reputation, and each time she went out with him, she went in some apprehension wondering if this time he would demand reward for his patience. But his advances never strayed beyond an arm around her waist or shoulders, and a good night kiss that stopped short of the kind of passion that might get out of hand.

Vonne presumed he took other women out, and she made no secret of the fact that she occasionally had a date with another man. Rina Robertson had taken her under her wing and had introduced her to a number of young people not connected with nursing. As a result, Vonne found herself involved in quite a hectic social life.

At the hospital Lorin remained aloof and critical, and despite the fact that she must have known they never went out together, she always seemed to watch Kirk with suspicious eyes when Vonne was around.

Vonne's encounters with Kirk continued to be fraught with tension. It seemed as though he would never come to terms with the fact that although she looked like Vicky, she was not Vicky. She saw in his eyes every time they met the suffering Vicky had caused, the resentment that he was unconsciously transferring to her. There were times when it hurt so much she thought she wouldn't be able to stand it much longer.

Breaking point came one morning when she arrived to find Lorin away. She had gone to the dentist for urgent attention to a broken tooth and did not expect to be in until after lunch. That meant that Vonne was delegated to take over temporarily, since she was the most senior in experience although the newest at the Bauhinia.

'You might as well get in some practice,' Kelly said. 'You'll probably be taking her place some time anyway.'

'I don't think so . . .' said Vonne, wondering what had prompted the remark.

Kelly explained, 'She's been hinting to her cronies that there may be wedding bells before long, and she's said that when she's married she doesn't intend to work and run a house and family. I thought she'd been looking a bit smug lately. I wonder if she really has nailed Kirk Leveson down at last.'

Vonne felt suddenly bleak. She was sure that Lorin

wasn't right for Kirk. 'It does rather sound like it,' she said, since Kelly seemed to require some response.

Any further discussion was curtailed by the demands of work. It proved to be what Kelly called a 'Murphy's Law' of a morning—everything that could go wrong, went wrong.

There was a mix-up over admissions and Vonne found that they were double-booked on one private room. While she was trying to sort that one out, Maggie, a nursing aide, dropped a vase of flowers in room four, slipped on the wet patch and fractured her wrist.

While Vonne was taking her along to Casualty, there were complaints from Recovery that they'd rung down twice to say two of Sister Kent's patients were ready to come back and no one had come up. Couldn't someone do something about the traffic jam up there?

The phone never seemed to stop ringing. Doctors breezed in and out, and Vonne battled to keep the essentials under control while beset with problems from all sides. In the midst of it all one of the patients who had just had an operation started vomiting as soon as she had had something to eat, and Vonne was the only nurse on hand to cope. She only had time for a fifteen-minute lunch break, and it was when she returned, that she was confronted with Kirk. His face was a thundercloud.

'Where's Sister Kent?' he bellowed.

'She broke a tooth and had to go to the dentist.' Vonne had expected her to be back before this.

'Who's in charge?'

Vonne drew herself up stiffly. 'I am.'

'You!' He sounded as though he thought someone must be crazy to allow it. 'And where the hell have you been?'

'Having my lunch.'

'It's half past two!' he thundered. 'Do you always take such a long lunch hour?'

Vonne bridled. He didn't know what time she'd gone

to lunch. And she wasn't under his jurisdiction anyway.

'I didn't go until after two,' she said calmly, although she was beginning to feel more than a little het up.

'You don't go to lunch at all if one of your patients needs you!' he raged.

'I'm sorry,' she faltered. 'Who . . . ?'

His voice was chilling, his look savage. 'I came to see Mrs Norman. She's on my theatre list for tomorrow—a myomectomy—and she's very nervous about it. She's never been in hospital before, never had an operation before.'

'Yes, I know that,' Vonne interrupted, wondering what he was getting at.

His eyes bored into hers. 'When I saw her she was hysterical. She's been lying there for hours, terrified out of her mind. She's sure she's got cancer even though it's unlikely, and I've told her so, but the point is she wanted someone to reassure her again. She was afraid to ring her bell, but she did ask one of the nurses, she says, to speak to the Sister in Charge to see if she could have a word with me before the operation. But she was ignored. No one went near her. You went and had your lunch and ignored her!'

Vonne took a deep breath. 'I—I didn't ignore her. I—I just forgot.' She recalled now that Maggie, before her accident, had flitted past her at one stage saying Mrs Norman wanted to see her when she had a minute, without explaining why. She had meant to go as soon as she could, but so much had been happening, it had slipped her mind.

'*Forgot?*' He made it sound like a major criminal offence. 'What kind of nurse are you to forget?'

Vonne cringed. 'It—it was rather hectic here this morning,' she muttered, wiping a hand across her brow. 'I—I'm sorry—I've had rather a lot of things on my mind . . .'

'Yes, I bet you have!' he said scathingly. 'Bart Webb

prominently, I shouldn't wonder.' His eyes were scalding.

'No!' He wasn't being fair.

'You spend most of your spare time with him, I hear,' the castigating voice went on. 'But if you can't keep your private life separate and it interferes with your work, you're scarcely fit to be a nurse.'

'That's a despicable thing to say!' From feeling thoroughly chastened, Vonne was suddenly incensed. 'It isn't true! I'm sorry about Mrs Norman—I admit it was an unforgivable lapse on my part, and my only excuse is that we've all had a rather torrid time here this morning. I know that isn't an excuse and that I should have been able to cope . . .' Her voice began to crack with emotion and fatigue. 'It isn't fair. I've been jilted too! I know what it's like. I haven't got over losing the person I loved either, but I'm not taking it out on anyone . . .' Her voice broke altogether and the tears of anguish and hopelessness burst through like a dam wall being breached. Dimly aware of the shocked amazement in his face, she pushed past him and fled to the nurses' room. Fortunately, no one else saw her.

Mercifully the room was empty. Vonne crossed to the window and stood there clutching the sill with desperate fingers until the knuckles were white. She dared not weep. Not yet. Not until she was off duty. She must not let anyone see she was upset. She had to get a hold on herself. She had to finish her shift somehow.

When the door clicked open, she turned, hoping whoever it was wouldn't notice how uptight she was. She had not expected it to be him.

'Vonne . . .' He came straight across the room to her and clasped her shoulder. It was a gesture of pure compassion. 'Vonne—I'm sorry.'

She couldn't hold back now. She slumped into his arms and wept against his crisply starched white coat. He patted her shoulders soothingly.

She regained control of herself and looked up at him.
'I think the best thing I can do is see the DN and resign.'

'You can't do that!' Kirk objected with surprising
vehemence.

He pulled her hard against him and she could feel his
heart beating as erratically as her own. He started to say
something more, but the sound of the door opening
startled them both and they drew apart automatically,
turning to see who it was.

'Kelly said you were both in here,' said Lorin Kent in a
voice of extreme displeasure. She glanced from one to
the other with deep suspicion and her gaze rested longest
and most accusingly on Vonne.

'Oh—Lorin! I didn't think you'd be coming back
now,' Vonne murmured rather lamely.

Lorin's eyes flashed and she favoured Vonne with a
sarcastic smile. 'I can see you didn't! And it would seem
that it's just as well I did.'

CHAPTER SEVEN

VONNE did not drive straight home that evening. She felt so on edge she had to calm down first, so she went up to East Point to watch the sunset. It wasn't very spectacular as there was too much cloud. The sky was almost as grey and depressing as her thoughts. Hardly anyone else had thought it worth the trouble to be there and she was almost alone.

She sat in the car and stared out across the Timor Sea towards Indonesia and Singapore. Very soon she would be winging her way in that direction once more. She had meant what she had said to Kirk that afternoon.

It was clear to her now that to remain any longer was unfair to Kirk. Besides, it was impossible for her to do her job efficiently when all the time she was tense, and when every encounter with Kirk was an ordeal. She simply couldn't bear any longer that look behind his eyes of longing and disappointment and frustration because she wasn't Vicky. If only she had realised it would be like this, she would never have agreed to come, however hard Vicky had pleaded.

Tomorrow, Vonne decided, she would talk to John Langham as soon as she came off duty, if he could see her then. If necessary she would tell him the truth about why she felt it imperative to break her contract. After all, he was a friend of Kirk's, and he knew about the broken engagement. He ought to understand.

Vonne felt easier in her mind once she had reaffirmed this decision to herself. The hardest part would be telling Diana, but she too would surely understand. She would want what was best for Kirk.

If Diana thought Vonne was rather subdued that

evening, she did not remark on it. Vonne hoped she would put her preoccupation down to tiredness. Several times, though, it was on the tip of her tongue to tell Diana that she had made up her mind to leave Darwin as soon as possible, but each time she checked herself. She owed it to Mr Langham to speak to him first.

It was still early when she pleaded tiredness and went to bed. But she was not weary enough to sleep immediately. She lay awake half the night mulling it all over in her mind, and in the morning she felt emotionally drained.

She had not changed her mind, however. Her resolve still stood, even though the prospect of broaching the subject with John Langham did not greatly appeal. As soon as she was able to do so without being overheard, particularly by Lorin, Vonne rang the DN's office and made an appointment with his secretary to see him as soon as she came off duty.

'You can come along earlier if you like,' Sue Gilmour offered. 'Lorin can spare you for half an hour, surely.'

'I'd rather wait until I finish,' Vonne said hastily.

'Just as you like,' said Sue amiably. 'See you then.'

The day dragged interminably for Vonne. For once the wards were quieter than usual. Yesterday's panic was history now, and the only reminder of it was Lorin's caustic remark:

'It seems I can't even have a tooth out without the wards turning into a shambles!'

Vonne endeavoured to keep out of her way as much as possible, but she still managed to have a brush with her. Over, of all people, Mrs Norman.

Vonne felt very guilty about her neglect of the previous day, so she made a special point of going in to see the patient, who was in a private room, as soon as she could after the morning's urgent tasks had been completed.

Nothing had been said about her at briefing, so presumably she had not presented any problem to the night staff. Vonne did not mention what had occurred yesterday. If Lorin was to find out that she had incurred Kirk's wrath over Mrs Norman, then it was up to him to tell her, she thought.

When Vonne went in to see her, Mrs Norman was sitting up in bed, reading a magazine. She looked a little flushed and her eyes conveyed a slight tension.

'Good morning, Mrs Norman,' Vonne said brightly. 'Have you got everything you need?'

The patient smiled shakily. She was making a determined effort to be cheerfully normal. 'Everything except breakfast!' she said in a quavery voice.

Vonne glanced at the 'nil orally' sign clipped to the end of her bed and chuckled sympathetically. 'I know —it's awful not being allowed to eat anything for hours before an anaesthetic, isn't it?'

Mrs Norman nodded. She looked hard at Vonne for a moment, then said rather sheepishly, 'I suppose you know I was a bit of a nuisance yesterday.'

Vonne pretended surprise. 'I'm sure you weren't.'

Anxious grey eyes met hers valiantly. 'I was—I didn't mean to make a fuss, but I couldn't help worrying— and then Dr Leveson was so kind about it, so reassuring, that I felt such a fool for wasting his time. It's just that . . .'

Vonne squeezed her hand comfortingly. 'There's absolutely no need for you to worry about a thing, Mrs Norman. You've got the best gynaecologist in town, and it's a very simple operation, nothing to fret about at all. It'll all be over and you'll be sitting up here having your tea before you know what's happened.'

Mrs Norman clung tightly to her hand. 'I know it's silly to be afraid.'

Kirk's reassurances had soothed her only temporarily, Vonne realised. Despite the brave front she was trying to put on, Mrs Norman was still very uptight. She rushed on apologetically, 'Dr Leveson said he'd try to have me listed early, but I don't want to be a nuisance. He's such a kind man, isn't he? He must be very busy, but he stayed for half an hour talking to me, a silly old woman who was all upset over nothing.'

'Not over nothing,' said Vonne gently. 'Having an operation is an ordeal, Mrs Norman, especially the first time. You're no different from anyone else.'

'But I'm so nervous!'

Vonne squeezed her hand. 'So are most people before an operation.' A thought occurred to her. 'Aren't you a bit lonely in here all by yourself? If you were in one of the other wards with company you might feel a lot easier. It helps to have someone to talk to, and it makes the time pass more quickly. There are three or four other ladies having similar operations to yours today.'

She spoke tentatively, looking keenly for a reaction. Mrs Norman had after all booked a private room, but people sometimes did that thinking they would prefer privacy, and then found it rather lonely and boring.

The patient considered briefly, then said a little wistfully, 'It's my own fault, really—although it was my daughter who persuaded me to have a private room. I wouldn't want to be a trouble—it's only for a few hours, after all . . .'

Vonne crossed her fingers, hoping that there was still a bed available in the five-bed ward. She had not been told of any new admissions this morning, but anything could happen. There were often emergencies requiring a bed right away. 'Would you like me to ask Sister if you can go into room four?' she asked. 'I think there's a spare bed there.'

Mrs Norman instantly brightened. 'Well, if it wouldn't be too much trouble, perhaps . . .'

'I'll see her straight away,' promised Vonne, relinquishing the nervously fluttering hand, and hurrying out.

Lorin was not in her office. Vonne asked Kelly if she knew where she was.

'She said she was going to see the DN,' said Kelly, and grinned. 'To report us for unruly behaviour, I dare say!'

She might well be reporting her, Vonne thought, remembering only too graphically how Lorin had caught her in Kirk's arms. What had she deduced from that little scene—that she was enticing him?

'Is there still a spare bed in room four?' she asked Kelly.

Kelly nodded. 'Yep. Why?'

'Mrs Norman's lonely. She was upset yesterday about her operation and she's still very nervous. I thought it might help if she had company instead of brooding on her own.'

Kelly nodded agreement. 'You want to move her in there?'

'I was going to ask Lorin if that would be OK.'

Kelly pulled a face. 'If I know her, she'll find some excuse why not. If you think it's a good idea, do it, and tell her later. Fait accompli. She won't insist on moving her back, it would make her look silly.'

Vonne was doubtful of the wisdom of doing it without Lorin's approval, but thought, 'Well, since I'm resigning anyway, I've nothing to lose.'

She checked out the spare bed and found it ready for occupancy. When she told Mrs Norman she could move if she wanted to, the patient's delight was justification enough for the decision.

Vonne helped the patient into her dressing-gown and said, 'Don't worry about your things. I'll bring them along in a minute.'

It only took a few minutes for Vonne to install Mrs Norman in the other ward, and introduce her to the patients already there. Two had already had operations, and two were due for theirs that day. One was to have a myomectomy too. Vonne was gratified by the almost instantaneous lessening of tension in Mrs Norman's face at having sympathetic company. A short time later, coming out of the store-room, Vonne came face to face with Lorin. With her was Kirk. Both looked slightly mystified, and Lorin asked suspiciously, 'Where's Mrs Norman?' in a tone that suggested Vonne might have accidentally mislaid the patient. 'She's not in her room.'

Vonne avoided Kirk's gaze. 'She's in room four now.'

'Room four?' echoed Lorin, with raised eyebrows. 'But Mrs Norman is supposed to be in a single room. What in the world . . . ?'

With a fleeting glance at Kirk, Vonne said quickly, 'Yes, but she was—er—rather upset yesterday about her operation. Dr Leveson reassured her, but she's still rather nervous, and when I suggested she might feel better in a ward with other people to talk to, she jumped at the idea. Luckily there was a bed vacant in room four.' She took a deep breath and plunged on, 'So I moved her.' Again she glanced at Kirk to try and gauge his reaction, but the expression in the greeny-gold eyes might have been disapproval or it might not. There was no doubt about Lorin's reaction, however. She was outraged.

'You mean you shifted her—of your own accord —without reference to me?'

Vonne moistened her lips. 'I didn't know how long you were going to be, and I was afraid she was on the verge of becoming hysterical again.' She chanced another quick look at Kirk, but his expression hadn't altered. She wasn't even sure he was listening.

Lorin's mouth was hard, her voice icy. 'It seems, Nurse Lothian,' she said pointedly, 'that being in charge for a day has gone to your head. May I remind you that you are not in charge today! If a patient is to be moved, I will decide. I think . . .'

Kirk cut across what she was about to say with, 'I saw Mrs Norman yesterday, as Vonne explained, and she was in a very upset state. I confess it didn't occur to me to move her into a ward where she would have company. Nurse Lothian should be commended for thinking of it.'

To Vonne's astonishment there was a glimmer of a smile creeping up his face, and the warmth in his eyes was for her. Her heart did a peculiar somersault. It was ridiculous how badly she had wanted that, how much it meant to her that he was pleased with her. It made the fury smouldering in Lorin's eyes of no consequence at all.

Sister Kent muttered sulkily, 'It would nevertheless be preferable, Nurse, if you would consult me before taking the law into your own hands.'

Kirk added blandly, 'But we must be careful not to stifle initiative in our nurses. After all, most of them have ambitions to be Sisters themselves.'

Ignoring this, Lorin enquired haughtily, 'Am I to assume you want Mrs Norman to remain where she is now when she comes back from Recovery?'

'Certainly,' Kirk rejoined. 'And I'll just pop in and have a quick word with her now. I want to let her know she's first on the list.' He glanced at his watch and gave them both a wry smile. 'Must hurry—I've got a surgery waiting for me!'

He went in to see Mrs Norman, Lorin accompanying him. Vonne took a deep breath and heaved a sigh of relief. An odd feeling was stealing over her, like some kind of quick-acting tranquilliser, that she couldn't identify, except that its cause was Kirk.

At last Vonne's shift was over and the moment of truth had arrived. Long before the end of the day her heart had begun to flutter apprehensively every time she thought of the interview to come, and her mind had only been half on what she was doing. Nevertheless, she managed to finish her shift without any further brushes with Lorin.

When Mrs Norman came back from Recovery, she

was almost perky, and showed no signs of any adverse reaction to the anaesthetic she'd been given. Vonne looked in to have a word with her before the shift changeover. She was sitting up and chatting about her grandchildren to the patient in the next bed. She brought out snapshots which Vonne passed back and forth between the beds.

To Vonne she said, 'I didn't think I'd be back on deck so quickly!'

Only a faint shadow underlay her look of relief now that it was all over. 'Of course I won't know for sure that everything's all right until the pathology report.'

'That'll only be a couple of days,' Vonne assured her. 'And it's just a precaution. Yours was a straightforward case of non-malignant fibroids, Mrs Norman, I'm quite sure.'

'That's what Dr Leveson told me,' she agreed, and with a smile, 'I really am trying not to worry!' She clasped Vonne's hand and said softly, 'Thank you so much, dear, for letting me come in here. I feel so much happier.'

Vonne was glad her idea had worked. It was a small thing, but it helped to boost her confidence in herself as a nurse, a confidence that had been eroded somewhat lately.

John Langham had the look of a man expecting trouble when Vonne knocked and entered his office after Sue Gilmour had checked via the intercom that he was ready to see her. He rose to greet her, a rather speculative smile preceding his words.

'Come in, Vonne—take a seat.' His shrewd gaze swept over her neatly uniformed figure and rested on her face. His eyes narrowed a little as though he didn't like what he saw there. 'Now, what's the trouble?' He was very disturbed by the strain evident in the pretty face before him. Girls like Vonne Lothian didn't specially request interviews unless there was something very important on their minds.

Vonne sat down in the visitor's chair nearest his desk and dispensing with formality he perched on the edge of the desk and folded his arms across his chest expectantly. She swallowed hard, searching for the right opening words, but her mouth was dry and the words she had rehearsed seemed to have got out of order.

At last she said, 'I'm sorry to bother you, Mr Langham—and I do feel rather terrible about this, but I—well, the fact is, I've come to ask if you will release me from my contract.'

This he had not expected. He leaned towards her, astonished. 'Release you? But why, Vonne? What's the matter?'

'P—personal reasons,' she muttered, although she knew he probably wouldn't let her get away with such a lame explanation.

'Homesick?' he queried with a smile.

She couldn't lie although it might have been convenient to. 'No, it's not that . . .'

'Hadn't you better tell me what it is?' he urged. 'I can hardly let you break your contract on the strength of an excuse as vague as "personal reasons", unless you can convince me it's so private I'm not entitled to know.' Several possibilities were running through his mind, but he would have been surprised if any of them had been Vonne's reason. A warm smile broke across his kindly face. 'I can keep secrets, you know, Vonne. Whatever you tell me will go no further, you can depend on that. Besides, I might be able to help.' When she didn't immediately answer he went on, 'I saw you out with Bart Webb one evening. Nothing to do with him, is it? You haven't got too deeply involved?'

Vonne was quick to deny it. 'No, it's nothing to do with Bart.' She sucked in a quick breath. 'It's because of Kirk.'

'Kirk!' His eyebrows flew up. He was jumping to the wrong conclusions, she saw at once, and she hastened to explain.

'Kirk and my sister,' she said.

His brow creased. 'I don't quite see—I mean, I know the engagement is off . . .'

'I don't know if you are aware,' said Vonne, finding that the words were coming together at last, 'that Vicky and I are identical twins. I'm afraid it didn't occur to either of us that this would make it extra difficult for Kirk. But it obviously has. He—he can't come to terms with losing Vicky because of my being here, looking exactly like her, and reminding him of her all the time. Sometimes I'd swear he thinks I *am* her, and then when he realises I'm not, he . . .' She broke off. She didn't want to openly accuse Kirk of harassing her.

But John Langham was astute. 'You mean he sometimes takes it out on you because you're not your sister?'

'Something like that,' Vonne admitted miserably. Anxious to get it over with, she rushed on, 'It's not his fault. He can't help being a bit confused. But it's a strain for both of us, and I feel it would be easier for him if I wasn't around.' Her troubled brown eyes pleaded with him. 'I shouldn't have come in the first place. I should have realised what might happen. I really can't stay, Mr Langham, it isn't fair to Kirk.'

John Langham did not answer immediately. It was a dilemma he had never encountered before. He regarded her thoughtfully, not entirely convinced by what she had said, yet acknowledging that it could be a possibility. Kirk had suffered a severe blow, and emotional reactions were often unpredictable.

'A problem, Vonne, a problem, I admit,' he said at last. 'But you're an excellent nurse and I'm loath to lose you so soon.'

'But I'm not,' Vonne put in desperately. 'Not lately —that's part of the trouble, Mr Langham. I'm so on edge I can't do my work properly. I'm jittery all the time, and that's not good for the patients.' She added dully, 'As Sister Kent could tell you.'

John Langham smiled at her. 'Not if my own observations are accurate, and Kirk's.'

'Kirk's!' Vonne was astonished.

'Oh, yes. He's mentioned several times how quick and intelligent you are, and that you have a pleasant manner with the patients.' He ignored her embarrassment and went on, 'What's more, little comments reach me from the patients themselves from time to time. I have my ear to the ground, Vonne. I need to know what's going on all the time in the hospital. You do not, however, so far as I can gather, get on very well with Sister Kent.'

Vonne bit her lip. 'I do try to . . .'

He nodded sympathetically. 'I'm not saying it's your fault. I suspect she may have rather personal reasons for being less than friendly towards you, which you are also no doubt aware of. A pity, but we're all human, Vonne, and less than perfect.'

'But there's no need for her to be jealous,' Vonne blurted out defensively, then wished she hadn't. She added, 'That doesn't worry me overmuch, Mr Langham. I've worked with more difficult people than Lorin. It's because of Kirk that I must leave.'

The DN, however, was not ready to agree with her. He said, 'I believe there could be some truth in what you've said, Vonne, and I'm sympathetic—towards you and Kirk—but I have the hospital to think of, and the patients. You did agree to work here for twelve months with an option to renew after that.' His kindly features were stern.

Vonne moistened her dry lips. 'I know.'

He stood up and looked down at her contemplatively. 'Vonne, I don't think I can give you an answer right away. I want to think about it. I can't stop you just walking out on us, of course, but I hope you won't do anything hasty. I'll talk to you tomorrow when I've thought it over.'

Vonne rose. She was disappointed. She felt sure he wouldn't let her go. 'I'm sorry,' she said, 'I've taken up enough of your time.'

He opened the door for her, and detained her briefly with a fatherly hand on her shoulder. 'I'll let you know.'

Which meant no, Vonne thought dismally, as she walked to her car. The choice would be up to her then—leave regardless, without hope of a reference, or stay and hope that time would improve matters.

'What am I to do?' she whispered desperately, as she slid behind the wheel. 'He doesn't understand how serious it is.' She was convinced that John Langham thought she was exaggerating, or that not getting on with Lorin was the real problem.

Diana was home early. 'You look all in,' she said with concern as Vonne came in. 'Hectic day?'

'It was a bit,' Vonne admitted, hoping she wouldn't ask for details.

'I've got to go out tonight,' said Diana. 'Red Cross meeting and dinner afterwards. I forgot to mention it this morning. Unless you're going out too, there's a casserole you can heat up.'

'You shouldn't have bothered,' Vonne protested. 'You ought to let me get my own meals. You spoil me!'

Diana scoffed. 'Rubbish! You cook almost as often as I do. I've never had it so good! I don't mind admitting I'll be sorry to lose you when those units are finished.' She added a little wistfully, 'I suppose you must go . . .' and when Vonne was stuck for a reply, added apologetically, 'Of course you want your own place and privacy. I'm just being selfish. I have so enjoyed having you here, Vonne.'

'And I've enjoyed being here,' Vonne said sincerely. If it hadn't been for Kirk she would have enjoyed it so much more.

'I suppose it won't be long now before the new building is finished?'

'Very soon, I think,' said Vonne, but did not add that she might not be moving into a unit at all. It would all depend on what John Langham said tomorrow, and if he said no, whether she could ignore her conscience and break her contract regardless. She had a conscience about Kirk, too.

Vonne was pleased to be alone for the evening in the circumstances. She was not hungry, so she did not re-heat the casserole; it would do for tomorrow. She nibbled at some biscuits and cheese, feeling edgy and unsettled. She tried to watch television, but could not concentrate on the programme.

When she heard the key turn in the front door, she knew it was too early for Diana to be returning. Her heart somersaulted. The only other person who had a key and walked in whenever he chose, and had surprised her before, was Kirk. Apparently he did not know that his mother would be out this evening.

He came straight into the living-room, and paused, impressively tall and broad-shouldered, with that loose-limbed look that characterised him even when he was standing still. His presence was always a commanding one, but to Vonne this evening, more disturbing than ever. Her heart was skipping along at an alarmingly hectic pace.

'Good evening, Vonne.' His tone was warm, his eyes searching.

'Diana's out.' Nervousness made her sound curt. 'It's a Red Cross do tonight.'

'Yes, she told me,' he said, and as Vonne stifled a little gasp of surprise, 'I didn't come to see Mother, I came to see you.'

Colour flooded her cheeks, and deepened when he said, watching her closely, 'I've just been torn off a strip by John Langham.'

Vonne was mortified. Her whole body seemed to freeze as she waited for him to speak again. Unable to meet his eyes, she stared at the television screen. Kirk strode over to it.

'You're not really watching that rubbish, are you?'

Mutely, she shook her head and he switched it off. 'You wouldn't by any chance have some coffee left in the pot?'

Vonne got up eagerly. 'I—I can soon heat it up,' she faltered, and escaped thankfully to the kitchen. She switched on the percolator and took down a cup and saucer with shaking hands. She clattered it on to the bench and then stood clutching the edge of the worktop till her knuckles whitened as she tried to gain a grip on her emotions.

She was pouring the coffee out when Kirk sauntered in. He opened the refrigerator. 'I haven't had a meal yet,' he complained, surveying the contents of the well-stocked fridge.

Automatically, Vonne offered, 'Would you like me to make you something?'

He closed the refrigerator door with a decisive thud and gazed fully into her face. 'Presently, perhaps. I'm not very hungry, and first there's something I want to say to you.'

'Kirk, is this necessary?' she put in hastily. She pushed the cup of coffee across the worktop towards him. 'Wouldn't it be better just to let it be? I can guess what the DN said to you, although he promised me our talk would be confidential. I wish he hadn't—I didn't want you . . .'

He ignored the coffee and caught her anxiously fluttering hands and held them still. His warm fingers interlaced tightly with hers and his touch sent shock-waves reaching to depths never before plumbed. The expression in his eyes was unreadable.

'You can't leave because of me,' he declared firmly.

'John would never forgive me if you did!'

Vonne did not know what to say.

He said, 'I'm sorry if I've been abrasive with you sometimes.'

'Kirk, I . . .' Vonne was totally at a loss.

He looked apologetically rueful. 'I know I'm like a bear with a sore head at times. I do a fairly stressful job, Vonne. We all have off-days.' He was sinking his gaze deeply into her face as he spoke, but she didn't believe a word of what he was saying. 'I didn't realise you were so sensitive.' He clasped her two hands between his large palms and absently moulded them. Warm currents ran through Vonne's body, and words died in her mouth. Worse, she could feel tears threatening.

There was deep compassion in his eyes as he went on, 'Vonne, my dear, I had no idea—Vicky never told me—that you'd been jilted. I'm so dreadfully sorry. It never occurred to me that you were tearing around with every male who invited you out because your heart was broken. I—I thought that was just the way you were.'

His sympathy was almost too much to bear. Especially as she suddenly knew that the real reason she was desperate to leave Darwin was a thoroughly selfish one. She was falling in love with Kirk. Ironically, it had begun that night he had kissed her at his and Vicky's engagement party. Despite her feelings for Leith at the time, something cataclysmic had happened that night. She had smothered it before it had had a chance to grow, but now finally it had to be acknowledged.

Kirk said persuasively, 'There's no reason why you should leave on my account. I hope you won't hold my irritation yesterday against me, or any other time I've snarled at you. I got quite a stern lecture from John for upsetting one of his best nurses! My name will be mud if you leave.' He tightened his grip on her fingers and the effect on her senses was to make her want to throw herself into his arms. 'After all, I arranged for you to come, so you're my responsibility. I should feel I'd let you down.'

Vonne swallowed painfully. She must extricate herself from physical contact with him before she was overwhelmed by emotions she must not show. She wriggled her hands free, saying, 'I feel a bit of a fool now—Mr Langham must think I am.' The DN had obviously not told Kirk what she had said about her resemblance to Vicky. He didn't believe it, she felt sure, and Kirk would have hotly denied it anyway, since he was probably not aware of it himself.

'Far from it. I'm the one he thinks a fool!' said Kirk.

Vonne looked at him helplessly.

'What would you like to eat?' she asked, anxious to get off the subject. 'What about an omelette? That won't take long.'

'That would be fine,' he agreed. 'Any mushrooms?' He smiled engagingly, his face relaxed now, and to Vonne suddenly more handsome than ever. 'Mother tells me you're quite a handy little cook,' he said. Vonne found herself caught for a moment in a spellbinding gaze. Kirk grabbed her shoulders and kept her facing him. 'You won't do anything hasty, will you, Vonne? You'll give me a chance . . . to make amends?' The new softer expression in his eyes only made her own feelings all the harder to control. And the last thing she wanted to do was to fall in love with her sister's ex-fiancé.

'I—I suppose so,' she agreed reluctantly.

'Good girl!' He bent his head and dropped a kiss on her forehead.

CHAPTER EIGHT

IN the end Vonne was left with the feeling that she'd made a bit of a fool of herself, even though she wasn't convinced that she had been completely unjustified.

When John Langham sent for her next morning, he apologised for speaking to Kirk. 'I couldn't see how else to tackle it,' he confessed. 'I don't want to lose you. He took my dressing-down very well. I didn't mention what you said about believing your resemblance to your sister presents a problem, because I'm not at all sure that it is, my dear.'

Vonne wanted to ask how he could be so sure, but she didn't. She could hardly tell him about those intimate moments with Kirk and the way he constantly looked at her, which were the only backing for her conviction.

John Langham said, smilingly, 'And I've got some good news for you today. The builders tell me that the new units will be ready to move in to in about two weeks' time.'

There was further good news to come a day or two later when new rosters were posted, and Vonne found that she had been relocated to a men's ward. She felt that this was not coincidental, but John Langham's way of giving her the benefit of the doubt and removing her as far away as possible from the orbits of both Kirk and Lorin.

While it was a relief to get away from the eagle eye and caustic tongue of Lorin Kent, and the inevitable encounters with Kirk, which now disturbed her for an entirely different reason since her feelings towards him had so dramatically crystallised, Vonne was a little disappointed. She had made good friends in Kelly and

Maggie in particular. She knew she would miss most Kelly's cheerful morale-boosting banter.

However, Julie Howard, the Sister in Charge of the men's wards, proved to be friendly and easy-going, and appreciative of having her. The other nurses, some of whom she already knew quite well, welcomed her, and so did the patients. A new face always caused a buzz of interest.

On her first morning, Vonne had to contend with wisecracks from both the young and the elderly. But it took several days for her to stop tensing every time a doctor appeared in case it was Kirk, and remember that gynaecologists did not visit men's wards!

She glimpsed Kirk in the distance sometimes, or having lunch if he happened to be at the hospital all day. Once she saw him sharing a table with Lorin, their heads close together, deep in discussion, and wondering if it was a personal rather than a medical topic they were so intent about, gave her a sudden hollow aching feeling inside.

As John Langham had promised, within a fortnight Vonne and a number of other nurses who had all been living out were about to occupy the eight new units. On the day of moving, Vonne had mixed feelings. She had enjoyed living with Diana Leveson, and was in many ways sorry to leave the house in Seaford Street, but she was also relieved because she was likely to see even less of Kirk now. Not that she ever did see much of him at Diana's, but the fact that he had surprised her there a couple of times kept her constantly on a knife edge.

When she was about to depart, she gave Diana the small gift she had bought as a thank-you for all her kindness—a Chinese silk picture of a bird. Diana was delighted and thanked her with tears in her eyes.

'Vonne, you shouldn't have!' she exclaimed. 'It's beautiful—it must have cost you a lot . . . Oh, dear, I am going to miss you!' She had spontaneously hugged her.

'Don't!' begged Vonne, 'You'll make me cry!' Which she was doing already.

They both wept a little, laughing at the same time at their foolishness, until Vonne dragged herself away to the car which was filled with her belongings and ready to go.

'Don't forget to come to the party,' Vonne reminded Diana as she got in.

Diana promised, 'I certainly won't.'

The nurses held their house-warming party a few days later. The new quarters were ideally designed for a big party. The units were built on two floors around a central quadrangle, which was reached from the outside by a fancy wrought-iron gate which could be locked for security.

The upper floor units had balconies overlooking the courtyard, while the lower units had flagged patios. The central area was grassed with shrubs and a couple of palms placed strategically in it. It was an attractive set-up and everyone was delighted with it.

All the hospital staff who were not on night duty, as well as some of the doctors who sent patients to the Bauhinia, were at the party, and there was a sprinkling of friends and relatives not connected with the hospital.

Like most of the other girls, Vonne had splashed out on a new dress to celebrate the occasion.

Kelly exclaimed when she saw it, 'Wow! Where did that little bobbydazzler come from? London?' Eyeing Vonne admiringly in the softly clinging apple-green crêpe that moulded her curves and swirled from the hips to enhance her long shapely legs, she added, 'You'll have every man in the place trying to date you! Bart'd better look out!'

Vonne scoffed, 'Don't exaggerate! As a matter of fact I bought it right here in Darwin. It was a bargain!'

Kelly eyed the effect with a cheeky smile. 'Well, I

don't know whether it's what the dress does for you, or what you do for the dress, but you look terrific.' She threw Vonne a rather shrewd glance. 'Maybe you just look happier since you got out of Lorin's clutches. Or maybe being on the men's wards suits you!'

'We—ell,' said Vonne, playing along, 'male patients do a lot for the ego, don't they!'

Kelly was partly right, of course, she did feel a lot more relaxed now that she no longer had to contend with Lorin, but what contributed more to her calm was not constantly bumping into Kirk. It allowed her to keep her feelings under control, and she felt she was beginning to master them. He would be here tonight, but Bart would not. Bart had gone off on a few days' holiday. He had not vouchsafed any explanation for this sudden decision to take a break, and when she'd asked where he was going he had been evasive.

'Oh, I'll just wander off somewhere and unwind, I expect,' he had said.

One of the nurses had provided a stereo and records for dancing, so there was soon a lively scene in the courtyard, with couples circling the central lawn, using the patios as a dance floor. The party was soon in full swing and very noisy. Vonne wondered anxiously how much of it would carry to the hospital. She hoped they weren't disturbing the patients.

Diana arrived with Kirk. Diana was simply and effectively dressed in white with gold chains around her neck, and Kirk was casually smart in cream trousers and a dark tan shirt.

'I think the units are fabulous,' Diana enthused, when Vonne showed them over hers. 'A bit small perhaps, but very compact and comfortable. All you really need, I suppose.'

They went back downstairs and Vonne showed them where the bar was. A few minutes later, Diana was spotted by an old friend, one of the local doctors, and was whisked away to dance with him.

'Shall we?' asked Kirk, looking at Vonne with an oddly whimsical expression.

She could hardly refuse, although she knew it would play havoc with her emotions. It was a kind of exquisitely painful bliss being held in his arms, swaying to the slow rhythm of the music that was playing just then. Vonne tried to remain impervious to him, but it was hopeless, with his arms around her, his cheek brushing against her hair, and the sensuous music wrapped around them.

They talked a little, inconsequential small talk, and it seemed to Vonne that he was trying very hard to be pleasant to her. She would have liked to think that because they had both been jilted, he considered there was some special bond between them, but she dared not let such an idea run away with her. Naturally he was sympathetic. And contrite, too, it seemed.

Halfway round the courtyard, they encountered a group with Lorin, Kelly and one or two others, as well as a couple of young locums only recently arrived in Darwin. Lorin dragged at Kirk's sleeve and it was impossible not to join the group. Vonne caught a scorching look from Lorin, as though she had committed a crime in dancing with Kirk.

She knew that if Lorin made any of her pointed remarks she might flare up, so she mumbled something about having to help with the supper and slipped away.

The preparations for the supper were well under control—two or three of the kitchen staff from the hospital having kindly offered to take over the catering for the party—so Vonne went upstairs to the balcony and watched the proceedings from there for a while.

Suddenly she felt a return of the uneasy feeling she'd had lately that was nothing to do with Lorin or Kirk. It was because she hadn't heard from Vicky. That was not a cause for worry in itself, given that Vicky was a

notoriously erratic letter-writer, but deep down Vonne
had a growing conviction that something was wrong. She
had often wondered if, when they were far apart, she
would know instinctively, if her twin was in trouble; the
rapport between identical twins did sometimes amount
to extra-sensory perception. There had been many small
instances when they were little, but that might have been
simply because they were constantly together and there-
fore able to sense each other's moods more accurately.
Ten thousand miles was a huge distance, she mused. In
any case, it was probably only her imagination. She was
inclined to be a worrier.

As her gaze moved idly over the throng below, she
saw Kirk and Lorin dancing along the patio on the far
side of the courtyard. Lorin's face was tilted dreamily up
to his and she was clinging to him in a close languorous
way. When they drifted into the shadows and did not
reappear, Vonne felt a sharp pang in the region of her
heart.

A minute or two later a figure loomed at her side. It
was Kirk.

'What's this? Hiding?' he joked, with a quizzical
arching of his eyebrows.

Vonne was so startled she jumped. She had only a
moment ago seen him vanish with Lorin, and now he was
here beside her and there was no sign of the Sister.

'No—just seeing what you all looked like from up
here,' she managed to say in a light tone, while the blood
in her veins seemed to fizz with a strange kind of
excitement.

'And that takes over half an hour?' He was standing
too close to her and her nerve ends were tingling.

'How did you . . . ?'

'You left in such a hurry, I thought perhaps you were
unwell,' he said, searching her face intently. 'And when
I spotted you up here all by yourself, I thought I'd better
come up and see if there was anything amiss.' His eyes

reflected the party lights, but she could see real concern there, and was touched.

'That was thoughtful of you,' she said, 'but I'm quite all right. I was just coming back.'

'No hurry,' he said. 'They're setting out the supper now and we don't want to get killed in the first rush!'

'I ought to go and help,' said Vonne, not wanting to, but knowing she was foolish wanting to stay with Kirk.

'I think they can manage.' He seemed determined to detain her. 'I want to ask you something—a favour.'

She was taken aback. 'A favour?' She couldn't imagine what kind of favour he would ask of her.

'I'll be going to Walparoo next weekend. Would you come?' At her startled glance, he added with a slightly teasing smile, 'It will be perfectly proper—Mother will be coming too. And in any case, my manager and his wife live at the homestead.'

Vonne flushed. 'How would it be a favour?'

'I usually hold a clinic for local people when I go to Walparoo, and it's a help to have a nurse along. It's a long way to Darwin or Katherine for the people who live on the station, and a couple of other properties in the vicinity, so about once a month or so I have a surgery for them.'

'And you always take a nurse?' Vonne was dubious.

'Not always. It depends.' By which she guessed he meant whether his current girl-friend happened to be a nurse. But she wasn't his girl-friend. If anyone was, it was Lorin.

'Can't Lorin go?' It was out before she was aware of speaking.

His eyes narrowed. 'I haven't asked her to. Mother said you were keen to see a cattle station, and I thought you'd jump at the chance.'

Vonne gave a crooked smile. 'You mean, you're doing me a favour?'

He shrugged. 'If you insist on seeing it that way. But

that wasn't my intention. I'm expecting a fairly heavy demand for attention this trip because I haven't been there for a couple of months, and they tend to save up their problems unless there's something urgent enough to warrant a call to the Flying Doctor or a trip to town.'

Vonne was torn between a natural desire to see more of the country, and in particular a cattle station, and a reluctance to place herself in too close a proximity to him for a whole weekend. But if Diana was going . . .

Kirk was waiting for her answer with an intense look. 'I shall think you haven't forgiven me,' he said, 'if you refuse to come.'

Vonne smiled at him helplessly. A part of her longed to go for quite different reasons from those she was canvassing to herself, and he wasn't making it easy for her to refuse, especially looking at her in that appealing way.

'All right,' she said recklessly. 'Thank you for the opportunity. I hope I'll be useful.'

He clamped a large warm hand on her shoulder. 'Good girl!' And almost absently, as he had once before, he dropped a casual kiss on her forehead. 'Now, let's go and get some supper before it all disappears.'

During the following week, Vonne several times half made up her mind to tell Kirk she couldn't go to Walparoo after all, but before she had concocted a plausible excuse, Diana phoned to remind her and to tell her to bring a swimsuit.

'We'll go for a picnic to the billabong, and you can see the abandoned goldmine.' She chattered on enthusiastically and Vonne felt that she would have to stay committed.

On Friday morning, she was suddenly surprised to encounter Kirk in the corridor when she was taking a tray of specimens to the lab.

'Lost your way, Doctor?' she quipped facetiously,

since sudden encounters with him still put her off her stroke.

'No. I was coming to see you,' he told her. 'We're going to Walparoo this afternoon instead of tomorrow morning, if you can make it. I'll pick you up as soon as you like after you come off duty.'

Vonne was slightly put out by the unexpected change of plan, but she said, 'All right—can you give me half an hour to pack my bag?'

'Sure,' he agreed. 'There's no rush. We'll have plenty of daylight for the trip.'

Vonne was not quite ready when he arrived, having been delayed for a few minutes at the hospital. She sat him down with a drink while she completed her preparations. His presence in her flat, comfortably sprawled in her armchair, was disconcerting to say the least, and she wondered again at the wisdom of going to Walparoo with him. But it was too late to back out now.

She was feeling so confused by him that she did not realise until the car suddenly turned off into the airport, that this was not the way to Diana's.

She turned to Kirk, puzzled. 'Why are we going to the airport?'

He gave her a quizzical glance. 'That's where planes take off from.'

'You mean we're flying?' She had supposed he would be driving.

He grinned. 'Didn't I tell you? Surely Mother did . . . ?'

Vonne was quite sure neither of them had mentioned it. She said, puzzled, 'But surely there isn't . . .' and stopped, aware that what she had been going to say must be ridiculous. Of course there wouldn't be a service, which meant there was only one other explanation. 'You have your own plane?' she asked. Something else Vicky had never told her, she thought, if she even knew.

'Dad bought it a few years ago. Just before his last

illness, as a matter of fact. He was always keen on flying. He was a pilot during the war.'

'You fly it yourself?' queried Vonne.

'Is that such a surprise?' Kirk seemed amused.

'No—well, yes it is, I suppose. Not everyone has their own plane.'

He laughed at her astonishment. 'I don't fly as much as I'd like to, mostly only between Darwin and Walparoo. It's easier and quicker than driving. The roads are pretty rough out in the Never-Never.'

'The Never-Never?' Vonne echoed, intrigued by the curious name.

He parked the car and explained, 'That was what some of the early pioneers dubbed the country. One woman wrote a book called *We of the Never-Never*. Mother's bound to have a copy of it somewhere, and Mrs Gunn's other book, *Little Black Princess*. You must read them both. You'll love Bet-Bet, the little Aboriginal girl she writes about.' His hand rested lightly on her thigh. 'Come on, Mother will be waiting for us.'

Vonne looked across at the light aircraft lined up on the tarmac and wondered which one belonged to Kirk. A Boeing 727 was taxiing out from the commercial airlines terminal, some distance away.

Kirk was saying, 'Sometimes it's difficult to get to Walparoo during the Wet if floods cut the roads. It's rare, though, for our airstrip to be out of commission, so we can usually get in by air.' He added with a grin, and taking hold of her arm, 'You're not nervous, are you?'

'No—of course not!'

'I thought you looked a bit wary,' he said. 'Haven't you flown in a small aircraft before?'

'No, I haven't.'

'I can guarantee you'll enjoy seeing the great Outback from the air,' Kirk assured her.

Diana was waiting for them. 'Oh, good, you're on time,' she greeted them with a warm smile. 'You never know with doctors and nurses—anything can happen!'

A few minutes later, when Kirk had filed his flight plan and completed the necessary formalities, Vonne was securely belted into the seat beside his, with Diana behind them.

She felt rather nervous as they taxied out on to the runway and prepared for take-off. She was sure that Kirk was as good a pilot as he was a doctor and surgeon, but it was a little difficult to get used to him in the role of pilot.

There was silence as they sped along the tarmac gathering speed. Vonne could not help holding her breath as the grassy verges blurred alongside the runway, and her stomach turned over as the little plane's nose lifted and she felt the wheels part company with the ground.

Then, all at once, there was a delicious feeling of freedom as they climbed towards the clouds. It was totally different from flying in a jumbo jet. It was breathtaking to see the ground receding, the airport buildings diminishing and then, as they banked and levelled out, the whole city of Darwin spread out below. Vonne had not realised that flying could be so exhilarating. In a jumbo you were soon above the clouds and there was little to see, but this was a thrilling experience. She turned eagerly to Kirk, and he smiled at the childlike excitement in her eyes.

He said with a smile, 'All I have to do now is to bring her down again. Anyone seen the flying manual?'

'Kirk! Don't tease the girl!' Diana expostulated.

Vonne laughed and asked, 'How high are we flying?'

'About five thousand feet,' Kirk answered. 'How do you like it? Better than being catapulted from one air terminal to the next in an aluminium capsule?'

'I hate flying,' said Diana with feeling. 'The other sort, I mean. I love this.'

'I think—so do I!' said Vonne, gazing awed at the vast

empty spaces of the Northern Territory unfolding below them as they left Darwin and the glittering ocean behind.

The sun was setting when they descended towards the airstrip at Walparoo. To Vonne it seemed like the middle of nowhere. She stepped down from the plane and looked around her. There was no sign of a homestead.

Diana answered her unspoken query. 'The homestead's about a mile away. And here comes Jacob.' She added the explanation, 'Kirk's manager. His wife Dora looks after the house for us.'

Following her pointing finger, Vonne saw a cloud of dust approaching and deduced it was a vehicle. By the time the dust cloud had materialised into a Land Rover, Kirk had unloaded their luggage, his medical kit and a couple of cardboard boxes of supplies which Diana had brought, and was securing the plane against any sudden gusty weather.

A tall, grey-haired man got out of the Land Rover. He doffed his broad-brimmed hat and smiled a welcome. His curious gaze lingered for a moment on Vonne.

'G'day, Kirk,' he drawled. 'G'day, Mrs Leveson.'

'This is Vonne Lothian, Jacob,' said Diana. 'She's a new nurse at the Bauhinia, from England. She's come along to give Kirk a hand with the surgery and to take her first look at a cattle station.'

Jacob shook Vonne's hand firmly. 'Pleased to meet you. I hope you won't be too disappointed. There's not an awful lot to see on a cattle station.'

Vonne and Diana scrambled into the rear of the Land Rover while the men stowed their bags behind. Diana heaved a contented sigh.

'I love coming out here,' she said. 'I hope you will too, Vonne.' She made it sound as though she expected Vonne to be a regular visitor.

During the drive up to the homestead which was

concealed behind some low hills, Vonne could see little of the surroundings out of the side window because of the dust that swirled around the Land Rover. It also made her cough.

Kirk turned round and said apologetically, 'Sorry about the dust. We haven't had any rain for quite a while.'

'It feels as though it's been hot today, Jacob,' said Diana.

'Right. And it's going to be hotter, Mrs Leveson,' the manager replied.

'It's usually warmer here than in Darwin,' Kirk told Vonne, 'but not so humid in summer. In Darwin the temperature rarely rises above thirty-five, but here we can get highs of forty or more.' At her look he added with a laugh, 'But not this weekend, I hope!'

The Land Rover skirted a succession of low hills and then they were almost on top of the homestead. Its white roof stood out plainly amid surrounding trees. Jacob parked in the shade of the feathery canopy of a poinciana tree at the front of the house.

It was a large rambling house, made of stone, with a corrugated iron roof and wide shady verandahs. Creepers tangled in untamed profusion across the curved verandah roof and twined around the supporting posts. The only flowers that seemed to be flourishing in the garden were geraniums, which sprawled everywhere in a medley of scarlet, pink and white. The house looked very old.

Diana confirmed that impression. 'The original part of the house is over a hundred years old,' she said. 'It was originally built by Kirk's great-grandfather about the same time as Springvale, a famous homestead near Katherine. The first settlers drove their stock a thousand miles up from Adelaide. It must have been tortuous for men, horses and cattle.' She grimaced. 'I don't think I would have made a very good pioneer wife—I like my home comforts too much! How some of those women coped I'll never know.' She glanced around at Kirk and Jacob who were unloading their gear. 'Come on, let's leave them to it. We'll go inside and find Dora.'

The interior was a surprise. Vonne wasn't quite sure what she had been expecting—perhaps something rather austere and sparsely furnished. She certainly hadn't envisaged the cool, comfortable surroundings that greeted her. While the exterior of the house probably remained more or less as it had been for a hundred years, the interior had been carefully restored and furnished with pieces that reflected its colonial history. From the entrance hall, Vonne could see into the living-room on one side and the dining-room on the other.

Diana said, 'I doubt if the original inhabitants lived as comfortably as we do, but Bill and I wanted to be able to relax, so we made it as comfortable as we could without spoiling its original atmosphere.'

'You've succeeded wonderfully,' said Vonne, gazing round in admiration. 'It's the kind of house that makes you feel at home straight away.'

Diana seemed pleased. 'I'm glad you said that, Vonne. I want you to feel at home here.' She led the way through to the rear of the house where, in a huge kitchen, she called out, 'Dora! Are you there?'

Jacob's wife was just coming through the back door with a basket of eggs.

'Hello, Mrs Leveson!' she exclaimed, carefully placing the basket on the sink drainer. 'I've just been seeing to the chooks.' Her eyes flashed with curiosity as she ran them over Vonne, and Diana introduced them.

Dora said, 'I made up another room when you said you'd be bringing a guest. It's the one next to yours, Mrs Leveson.' To Vonne she said, 'It's nice to have you here, Miss Lothian. Let me know if there's anything you want, won't you?'

'Thank you very much,' smiled Vonne, adding, 'But please call me Vonne.'

Diana showed her to her room and the bathroom, then said, 'When you've settled in, come out to the verandah and have a drink. But take your time, dear. We don't watch clocks here. You'll be a bit busy tomorrow for a spell, but the rest of the time is for relaxing.'

Vonne crossed to the window and looked out. She could not see far beyond the creeper-laden verandah, but there were glimpses of outbuildings, the stark white trunks of ghost gums in the distance, and the skeletal framework of a windmill. The shadows were long and it would soon be dark.

Taking Diana at her word, Vonne did not hurry. She flung herself down on the patchwork quilt that covered the bed, to snatch a few moments of private pleasure in her surroundings. Already she could feel the tension ebbing away. There were unfamiliar sounds from outside—insects, the windmill turning—but they were distant, soothing sounds.

The roughcast walls were painted white and relieved by large colourful paintings of Outback scenes. Vonne studied them from her prone position for some minutes, but curiosity made her get up for a closer look. She deciphered the signature on one of the oils as W. Leveson. So Kirk's father had been an artist as well as a medical practitioner.

It did not take Vonne long to unpack and hang up the few clothes she had brought for the weekend. She arranged her toilet articles on the old-fashioned marble-topped dressing table, then slipped out to the bathroom for a quick shower. Afterwards, she dressed in navy-blue slacks teamed with a pale blue poplin top. She had been reluctant to come for a number of reasons, but now that she was here she was glad she had.

'Vonne, how lovely and fresh and cool you look!' exclaimed Diana, when Vonne emerged onto the verandah at last. Kirk was also there. He said nothing, but treated her to a long steady look that devastated her calm, and set her nerve ends tingling.

He rose and motioned her to a chair. 'A drink?' he invited, looking down at her, with an almost tender smile curving his mouth.

'I'd love something long and cold, please,' she said. 'I'm parched!'

'All that dust,' said Diana. 'Never mind—one of Kirk's Walparoo Specials will re-lubricate your throat!'

'It's mostly lime juice,' said Kirk, as he strode towards the door. 'It won't have you on your ear, I promise!'

Vonne laughed. 'I hope not, if you want me to be useful tomorrow.' He's trying hard to be nice to me, she thought, and a whole weekend of it is going to break me up. I was a fool to come.

While Kirk was fetching Vonne's drink, Diana said, 'We were just discussing Sunday's picnic. Do you ride, Vonne?'

'No, I'm sorry, I don't . . .'

'It doesn't matter. Old Marigold can take you,' and as Kirk returned, 'can't she, Kirk? Marigold refuses to go faster than a slow walk, so you'll be as safe as houses on her.'

Kirk handed a tall frosted glass to Vonne. She carefully avoided any physical contact with him. He chuckled and said, 'If Vonne's going to ride Marigold, we'd better start out extra early!'

Jacob strolled up at that point and sat on the edge of the verandah. Kirk handed him a beer and they began to discuss station matters, with Diana interposing a brief remark or question now and then. Vonne listened with interest to the conversation, and in the space of half an hour, learned a good deal about cattle stations and their management.

It was quite dark when they went in for dinner. Kirk said, 'I hope there'll be time to show you around tomorrow after we've got surgery out of the way. Although there isn't really a lot to see.'

'Where are all the cattle?' Vonne asked. 'I haven't seen one!'

He laughed. 'They do spread out a bit. We don't graze our stock up here like they do in England. The pasture wouldn't stand it.'

After dinner Diana and Vonne both helped Dora with the washing-up, and afterwards returned to the verandah where the men were still mulling over station matters.

'Let's go for a walk,' said Diana, and Vonne willingly followed her out into the cool night air.

The night was full of unfamiliar bush sounds and strange tangy fragrances. The sky was a glittering web of stars, and Diana pointed out some of the main constellations, including the Southern Cross.

When Vonne was startled by a distant eerily mournful animal sound, Diana told her it was a dingo. 'Dingos don't bark,' she said. 'They only howl.'

They circled the garden and when they returned to the verandah Jacob was saying good night. Diana yawned and said she was ready for bed too.

'But if you're not too tired, Vonne, I'm sure Kirk would like to put you in the picture for tomorrow.'

Kirk said at once, 'It's rather late and I'm sure Vonne is tired.'

Diana, however, seemed anxious to leave them together. 'Well, just a few minutes,' she said, and quickly disappeared into the house.

Vonne felt uncomfortable. She was sure that Diana was trying to matchmake, and that Kirk must also be aware of it. She sat down, and when Kirk didn't immediately speak, she said:

'I suppose your father used to see patients here too?'

Kirk came to life. 'Yes. It's been a kind of tradition since my great-grandfather's day. He was a GP and he often used to ride immense distances on horseback to see patients. There was no Flying Doctor when he first came to Australia.'

'You were going to tell me about what happens tomorrow,' she said, remembering why she had lingered.

'Yes, of course, I was forgetting!' he laughed. He explained briefly the routine for seeing patients, who, he said, would drift in throughout the morning.

'And now,' he finished, 'you'd better get your beauty sleep.'

Vonne started to collect up the empty beer cans and glasses on the table, but a strong hand closed on her wrist as she did so.

'Leave them,' said Kirk. 'I'll do it.' But he did not get up.

For a moment she was held captive, looking with a slightly startled expression into his face, whose expression she could not read. Then, with a purposeful movement, he slowly drew her down on to his lap and held her there firmly. Vonne's lips parted to protest, but his lips reached hers before any sound came out, and then it was too late. She could not resist the gentle pressure that insidiously aroused responses in her which flared up as wildly and uncontrollably as a grass fire when his kiss deepened. His hand warmed her spine with electrifying touches and, hardly aware she was doing it, she allowed her own hands to encircle his neck and the tips of her fingers to stray into his hair.

It was some moments before he ended the kiss and drew back so that he could look searchingly into her face. Vonne saw the deep longing and frustration in his eyes and was mortified. As it had been that first time in London, and the time he had caught her as she stumbled in Diana's driveway, his kiss had been for Vicky, not her.

'You're lovely,' he murmured, drawing her close, his mouth eager to claim hers again, and real desire beginning to smoulder in the tawny irises. It was hard to resist him, when she wanted more than anything to be in his arms, making love to him, but she managed to damp down the fires of her own desires sufficiently to mutter huskily, 'No, Kirk . . .'

His smile said he didn't believe she meant it. The gentle caressing of his hands was almost too much to bear, and when he said, 'Why not?' she was nearly not able to resist the appeal.

She scrambled away from him breathlessly. 'Good night, Kirk!'

He was still holding out his empty arms towards her and he gave a little disappointed sigh. 'Good night, Vonne,' he said softly, and she ran quickly inside before she changed her mind.

CHAPTER NINE

VONNE was woken early by the soft cooing of doves outside her bedroom window, and the loud impatient cht-cht-cht of a willie wagtail scolding one of the station cats. A light breeze stirred the curtain in front of the partly open window and a faintly spicy perfume from some flowering shrub or creeper in the garden drifted into the room.

Hovering between sleep and wakefulness, Vonne allowed her thoughts to dwell on Kirk as painfully as she had once thought of Leith. It was strange how insidiously it had happened. Leith's features were blurred now in her mind, and the agony of longing she had suffered at his rejection had miraculously vanished. What was in its place was a depth of feeling she had never felt for Leith, and she could only marvel at this discovery. It seemed that she must never have been in love with Leith.

Her feelings for him had grown out of sympathy, because he was disabled and his fiancée had rejected him. But surely her feelings for Kirk too had grown out of feeling sorry for him because Vicky had let him down. Perhaps, after all, it was only pity she felt, not love. Whatever it was, she thought bleakly, as she got up at last, she had certainly never been as deeply affected by a man as by Kirk.

She showered and dressed in the uniform she had brought, then went along to the kitchen. Dora was baking bread, and the aroma of freshly baked loaves made Vonne feel hungry despite her emotional turmoil.

'Good morning!' Dora greeted her cheerfully. There

was generous approval in her shrewd eyes. 'Did you sleep well?'

'Very well, thanks,' said Vonne, which wasn't quite true. She had lain for a long time wishing she was in Kirk's arms. 'Am I very late up?' she asked, hoping she was not going to make a bad impression.

Dora brushed the flour off her hands. 'Mrs Leveson is still in bed. She always has a lie-in the first morning here, and I don't blame her. She works hard in that shop.' She nodded meaningfully at Vonne. 'Nurses work hard too. You should have slept in longer.'

Vonne shook her head. 'I'm used to getting up early. Besides, patients are likely to start arriving at any time, Kirk said.'

Dora kneaded dough energetically and said, 'We had a call from a mining survey team that's camped about a hundred kilometres from here. Their medico had to go south on urgent family business and they've got a couple of blokes sick. They heard Kirk was here, so it looks as though you'll be doing a little trip this afternoon.'

As she was telling Vonne this, Kirk came through the back door. He greeted Vonne with a smile and a pleasant, 'Good morning!' while allowing his eyes to drift lazily over her. He looked less like a doctor this morning, she thought, observing the khaki short-sleeved shirt and trousers, and more like a rugged cattleman.

'Let's get breakfast out of the way,' he said briskly. 'We're going to be busy. Did Dora tell you about the survey team?'

'Yes, she was just telling me when you came in.'

'We'll fly out to them after lunch. There are about thirty men out there.'

They ate breakfast sitting at one end of the kitchen table while Dora finished her second batch of loaves and set them to rise. In spite of last night, Vonne felt an easygoing companionableness with Kirk, perhaps because he seemed more at ease with her than ever before.

He left the table first, giving her half an hour before he would want her in the room he used as a surgery. Vonne offered to wash up the breakfast dishes, but Dora shooed her out.

'I'll clear up later,' she said, 'when Mrs Leveson's had her breakfast.' She smiled warmly at Vonne. 'It's nice to see Kirk with a young lady again. It's about time he settled down and started a family.'

Vonne said quickly, 'Oh, I'm not Kirk's young lady, Dora, only a nurse at the hospital. I just came to help out this weekend.' She guessed that Dora did not know about Vicky.

Dora was unconvinced. 'Well, I dare say you will be his young lady before long if that's what he wants.' She laughed meaningfully. 'Watch out! Kirk is a man who always gets his own way—right from a little boy, he has . . .' She demanded bluntly, 'Do you like him?'

Vonne could only answer, 'Yes, of course.'

There was a small group of Aborigines waiting on the verandah when Vonne went into the small spare room that Kirk used as a surgery. They greeted her cheerfully and with the friendly curiosity she was to become accustomed to as the morning wore on. Everyone was keen to know all about her.

Kirk, in a white coat, was unpacking his medical bag.

'I have most things I need here,' he told her, 'and I stock up on the most used items each trip.'

'Do you enjoy being a GP for a change?' asked Vonne.

He grinned. 'Yes, I do. It was what I wanted to do most at first, and I did after I qualified, but later I had the urge to specialise.'

He showed her the cupboard where he kept instruments, dressings and medications, so that she could stack the fresh supplies away. Then he went on, 'They come here with all the non-serious ailments they can't treat from the first aid box with aspirin or Band-aids.

And I make sure that the children get their inoculations.'

'They're lucky you're a doctor,' commented Vonne.

'And I'm lucky to have a bunch of reliable people running Walparoo, as well as good neighbours who look out for my interests when I'm not around, even though we're not exactly next door in the ordinary sense.'

That people appreciated Kirk's service to them, Vonne soon discovered from the many comments made to her out of his hearing. She learned that he never charged anyone, and in fact refused to accept fees for consultations at Walparoo. She was glad she had turned down his offer of remuneration for the day.

The first patient was one of the Aboriginal stockmen who had a bad gash in his hand. He had ridden in from one of the outstations. When Vonne unwrapped the soiled bandage, she almost gasped aloud. The wound was festering and should have been attended to long since. He had injured it over a week ago, the man confessed.

Kirk was angry. 'This should have been properly attended to, Clarrie,' he admonished. 'Why didn't you go to the doctor in Katherine? Surely you could see it needed stitches.'

The man shrugged. 'It was OK. I thought it was getting better, but I was shifting a mob of steers a couple of days ago and it opened up. I don't know why it went bad on me then.'

Vonne was already preparing a kidney dish, antiseptic and swabs for cleansing the wound, and while Kirk was doing this, she prepared needles and sutures and laid out a sterile dressing pack ready for use. She anticipated that Kirk would want to give an antibiotic injection and also a tetanus booster, so she had the disposable hypodermics ready when he asked for them.

'Now,' said Kirk, having completed the job quickly and efficiently, with Vonne's help, 'I don't want you to do any heavy work for a couple of weeks, to allow that plenty of time to heal. You don't want to lose your thumb, do you? I'll tell Jacob to keep an eye on you, and in a fortnight I want you to go into Katherine to have the stitches out, unless I'm here in the meantime. Right?'

'Right, Boss!' said the man with a broad grin.

'And keep that hand clean,' ordered Kirk.

Afterwards he said to Vonne, 'I could have told him to come and see Dora every day for a clean dressing, but it would be a waste of time—he wouldn't bother. Fortunately he's healthy and the antibiotic should keep the infection under control.' He watched for a moment as Vonne put the used instruments in the small steriliser, then remarked, 'You must have done a stint in Casualty at some time.'

She turned, smiling, 'Most nurses do!'

'But they don't all use their heads,' he said. 'I like a nurse who doesn't have to be told every little thing, who knows what she's about, who isn't just a doctor's hand-maiden.'

Vonne burst out laughing. 'That's very unchauvinistic of you, Dr Leveson! I wish all surgeons were like you!'

Their eyes locked for a moment, and she caught a glimmer of suppressed desire in his. She abruptly turned away, afraid he would see her true feelings displayed too nakedly in hers.

A lot of children turned up, some patients, some not. Kirk showed Vonne where his supply of sweets was kept. 'That's what they come for!'

Vonne held several Aboriginal babies on her knees while Kirk gave triple antigen inoculations for whooping cough, tetanus and diphtheria, and observing the gentle way he dealt with the women and children she realised yet again why he was so popular a gynaecologist and obstetrician.

By lunchtime everyone had been attended to. Vonne had cleaned, sterilised and put all the instruments away, and had tidied up the room. She carefully locked up the drugs and put the key in her pocket to give to Kirk. She could hear him still talking to someone on the verandah, and she paused for a moment, listening, savouring the rich tones of his voice, and knew that this morning her love had grown, not diminished. She sighed deeply. If only his love could have been for her and not her sister . . .

Diana appeared at lunch, looking cool and elegant in beige jeans and a natural linen overblouse.

'I feel so guilty,' she said to Vonne. 'You've been working hard all morning while I've been loafing.'

Vonne said, 'It wasn't like work really, everyone was so friendly. I've really had a very interesting morning.'

Kirk joined them. 'This afternoon there'll be thirty-odd males ogling you. Will you find that just as interesting?'

'Intimidating perhaps!' laughed Vonne.

Kirk was anxious to get away straight after lunch, so Vonne hurried to her room to tidy up, then went to join him. As she came out on to the verandah to see Diana relaxing on a lounger she realised Kirk's mother did not intend to accompany them. At lunch she had got the impression she intended to.

'No, you two can cope better without me around.' She embarrassed Vonne by adding, 'Won't hurt you two to get to know one another a bit better!'

Kirk drove the Land Rover out to the airstrip where the plane waited. It was hotter now and the sky was perfectly clear except for a jet trailing a vapour trail across it, a reminder that despite the emptiness of the terrain, civilisation was not so very far away.

The flight to the geologists' camp did not take long. Vonne's eyes were on the ground all the way. Once she saw a cloud of dust on a dirt road, a truck going to or coming from somewhere. They passed over a homestead with a cluster of nearby buildings, all shimmering in the heat. A distant tiny figure on the ground looked up and

waved. A lump came into Vonne's throat at the thought
of the loneliness of living in such an isolated spot, but of
course the people who lived there probably weren't
lonely at all. Doubtless it was their chosen way of life and
they were happy with it.

The airstrip that had been bulldozed close to the
survey team's camp was rough and their landing was a
bumpy one. They were welcomed by a rangy, deeply
tanned man in a broad-brimmed hat. Vonne thought he
looked like a typical Australian until he spoke and she
was astonished to hear an English North Country accent
which sounded oddly accentuated out here in the bush.
He shook her hand warmly.

'Doug Wilberforce. How do you do? Hi, Kirk.'

'Vonne Lothian,' Kirk introduced her. 'From
England.'

Doug Wilberforce beamed. He was the geologist in
charge of the party, which had been working in the area
for a couple of years, surveying for minerals and oil. He
was eager for news of home, and chatted eagerly to
Vonne as they walked back to the camp.

Vonne had half expected to find a collection of tents
and few home comforts, but she discovered she was
wrong. The huts the men lived in were comfortably
furnished and air-conditioned.

'Oh, yes, we're quite civilised,' laughed Doug.
'Though we rough it when we're out doing surveys for
three or four days or so. This is the base camp and as
comfortable as we can make it. We've been here quite a
while, but we'll be moving on soon.'

Not all the men were in camp, but Vonne was, as she
had been warned, treated to some flirtatious glances and
once or twice she caught the tail end of a saucy remark.

'We were hoping not to have to bother anyone,' Doug
said apologetically. 'Phil's only going to be away a week.
But wouldn't it . . . Ted Barnes has to go and bust his
foot. Twisted it in a rabbit hole and it's up like a balloon.

We've done what we could, but I'm a bit worried in case there are any broken bones. We called the Flying Doctor, but they're having a problem with one of their planes. They said you were at Walparoo and might be able to come over and do them, and us, a favour.'

Kirk laughed. 'What it is to have mates in the Flying Doctor Service! And how did they know I was going to Walparoo? There must be a very efficient grapevine around these parts.' He turned to Vonne. 'If it's a fracture we might have to take the patient to Darwin.'

But there was no fracture, luckily. Ted Barnes had merely sustained a rather bad sprain. Kirk examined the swollen foot.

'No bones broken, but you'd better rest up for a week,' he advised, 'and then don't do any hundred-kilometre hikes for a while after that. If it gives you any trouble, you'll have to have it X-rayed, but I very much doubt that'll be necessary.' He went on, 'If you want to go back to Darwin, we can give you a lift out tomorrow. You can come to Walparoo with us overnight if you like.'

Ted shook his head. 'I don't think I will, thanks all the same. I'll be right. I've got some reports to write up, so I'll hang in here.'

'Make sure Phil takes a look at it when he gets back,' Kirk told him.

There were several other men who discovered minor complaints they wanted to consult the doctor about, one of whom was convinced he was about to go down with malaria. Kirk assured him he wasn't.

Doug said it was strange, they hadn't had much work for the medico on the team for weeks.

'We're generally a pretty healthy crew, but the minute he left everybody started getting something wrong with them.'

'Psychological,' said Kirk. 'Having a doctor around is like having a magic charm against evil, I guess.'

As a souvenir, Vonne was given a small piece of rock with what looked like gold glittering in it. Doug said, 'Best we can do, I'm afraid—pyrites—known as fool's gold!'

'I'll treasure it just the same!' Vonne assured him.

That evening, Vonne was careful not to be left alone with Kirk after dinner. She was tired in any case, and wanted to try and get a good night's sleep because Kirk had said they would set off early in the morning. She was apprehensive about riding a horse for the first time in her life, but both Kirk and Jacob assured her that Marigold was incapable of throwing anyone off.

'I hope I won't be the exception that proves the rule!' she joked.

She slept well and woke feeling refreshed and thoroughly rested. Yesterday had been a pleasantly companionable day, she reflected. Today could be just as enjoyable, especially as Diana would be along too. So long as she did not dwell on her own emotional conflict, and Kirk treated her as he had yesterday, all would be well.

She decided to wear jeans and a blue checked shirt for maximum comfort, not forgetting of course to wear her bikini underneath, as Diana had said they would go swimming.

Her pleasurable anticipation was dampened, however, when she went into the kitchen for breakfast and Dora told her, 'Mrs Leveson had a bad headache—she gets a migraine now and then, you know. She said to tell you she's sorry she won't be able to go with you today.'

Vonne was disappointed. Diana had seemed perfectly relaxed and well last night. But migraines did attack suddenly, she knew. 'Oh, that's a shame,' she said. 'Is there anything I can do for her??'

'No, you just go out and enjoy yourself,' said Dora. 'That's what she told me to tell you.'

Kirk, when he came in, said, 'These attacks always come on suddenly. She hasn't been able to discover exactly what it is that triggers them off yet, that is supposing there is something tangible.'

'She was looking forward to the picnic,' said Vonne.

His mouth quirked. 'You don't mind going alone —with me?'

'Should I?' she queried lightly. 'I didn't yesterday.'

He laughed softly, but added nothing to the remark.

When he helped her on to Marigold's back, his closeness had a dangerously electrifying effect, and she almost wished she had pleaded a headache too. She would be so much more alone with him today. She had the uneasy feeling that Diana had invented her migraine on this occasion because she wanted them to be alone.

It's no use her pushing us together, she thought, but desperately wished that it were.

'Hold the reins lightly—that's it,' said Kirk encouragingly, 'and just let Marigold take you. Keep your knees in firmly and your back straight. Great!'

As he left her to mount his own horse, Vonne felt more vulnerable than ever. She seemed to be so high off the ground, and Marigold seemed so enormous. Vonne ventured to pat the horse's neck. 'There, Marigold, all right, girl? You don't mind me on your back? And you're going to walk very gently, aren't you? You wouldn't want me to make a fool of myself in front of Kirk, would you?'

Marigold let out a breathy snort and tossed her head as though outraged at the very suggestion. One front foot stirred up dust restlessly and, startled by this sudden movement, Vonne stiffened, sure that humiliation was imminent.

'Easy, girl, Marigold,' she said hastily.

Kirk was fixing saddle bags on to his horse, Kulinia, whose name meant fire-stick, he told her. Kulinia was a fine gelding, with a glossy brown coat and a white star on his nose. He looked very frisky to Vonne. She hoped he wouldn't give Marigold ideas.

She was impressed with the ease with which Kirk leapt into the saddle, as though he spent his life on a horse, not in a surgery or an operating theatre.

He came up alongside her. 'All set?'

'I—er—think so.'

'Let's go, then. Marigold won't be hurried, I assure you.' He chuckled softly at Vonne's nervous expression. 'Relax—she's very docile. She'll look after you.'

Vonne endeavoured to do as he said, but as Marigold began to move forward, following Kulinia, she could not help being tense. She still half expected to fall off, but when after a few minutes she had not, she gradually began to relax. Kirk reined in and waited for Marigold to catch up and they continued side by side.

'You see, there's nothing to it,' said Kirk. His face was shadowed by his broad-brimmed hat, but Vonne guessed there would be a teasing look in his eyes. Something about the way he looked at that moment, the way he sat on his horse, straight-backed and assured, sent a wave of longing gushing through her, and she was glad of the white cotton hat pulled down over her curls that disguised her own expression.

'I'm sure there isn't, once you get used to it,' she replied tentatively.

'At least you're game. I bet you'd tackle anything.'

'Oh, I don't think I'm all that brave,' she protested.

'Perhaps your courage has never been tested.'

'I don't suppose it has,' she murmured reflectively, and a little shiver of apprehension ran through her. Would she be brave—really courageous, that was—if the circumstances demanded it?

It was very pleasant ambling along the bush tracks at Marigold's leisurely pace, and Vonne's confidence increased as she relaxed. Kirk talked intermittently about

the hospital, the mining survey camp, of Darwin and
Walparoo and a variety of other things, and the morning
passed companionably. Vonne wondered once, however, if he was deliberately keeping the conversation
impersonal.

Some distance from the homestead she at last saw
some cattle. There were several groups, standing and
lying in the shade of ghost gums or grazing on spinifex
and porcupine grass. They looked rather thin and bony,
and Kirk said their condition would improve when the
rains came and the pasture grew more lush. Soulful
brown eyes watched them curiously as they rode past,
but the animals did not move even when the horses came
close. They seemed perfectly at home quietly ruminat-
ing under the gum trees, but to Vonne they seemed out
of place. To her, cattle belonged in lush English fields.
She was thrilled when a group of kangaroos suddenly
bounded across in front of them and vanished into the
bush.

'Aren't they splendid!' she exclaimed. To her their
grace and beauty seemed to belong in this landscape and
to blend with it more naturally than the cattle's solid
presence.

'We'll be at the old gold diggings in a few minutes,'
Kirk told her after one rather long but companionable
silence.

Near the ruins they dismounted, and Kirk helped
Vonne down from Marigold, clasping her around the
waist and swinging her expertly to the ground. The force
brought her briefly up hard against him and they swayed
together for a moment, eyes locked in an exchange of
glances that made Vonne feel a trembling weakness
inside that was nothing to do with sitting in the saddle for
an hour or more.

Kirk released her abruptly, as though fearing to be too
close, and walked towards the ruins. There were only
the walls and chimney of a mud hut, and around it some

rusty machinery, overgrown by bushes and creeping plants.

'Was it a very rich mine?' asked Vonne.

'I believe it was in its heyday,' Kirk told her. 'It was only a small one, but apparently it yielded well for a time.'

'But it obviously hasn't been worked for a long time. The gold ran out, I presume.'

'That's right. At least it became uneconomic to transport the ore to the batteries.'

'It amazes me,' said Vonne, gazing around at the wild empty country, 'how anyone ever found gold or any other mineral. I mean, they didn't have the modern equipment those geologists have got, and they're not having instant success, are they?'

They walked around the site for some minutes and Vonne idly sifted through the heaps of dirt, which made Kirk tease, 'Hoping for a nugget somebody missed, are you?'

She laughed up at him. 'You never know!' and her laughter faded on the disturbingly penetrating look in his eyes. She glanced away quickly, afraid again of what he might see in her face.

They remounted and ambled further on until, in a narrow valley between cliffs of red and yellow rock, they came to the billabong. The bell tones of a pied butcher-bird lured them on, and parrots screeched across their path from tree to tree, vivid splashes of green and crimson against the blue sky.

The billabong nestled in a rocky depression between outcrops of rock. A wide limpid pool reflected the stark white trunks of ghost gums growing near its edge. Marigold and Kulinia both stopped and lifted their noses testingly into the air, and Marigold neighed softly.

Kirk said, 'The horses know this is a special place. And if you're imaginative you'll feel the presence of spirits here—Aboriginal Dreamtime spirits. It's part of a sacred site, but the billabong is not forbidden to us, so long as we respect its magic.'

'It's such a peaceful place,' Vonne murmured, 'I feel sure they must be benign spirits.' The butcher-bird's liquid notes rang like a carillon around the valley and Vonne caught Kirk's eyes, and the message in them made her nerve ends tingle. For once she did not even think of Vicky. She felt as though she had in some strange way been touched by magic.

He dismounted and helped her down as before, but this time their bodies did not touch. There was only the slightest hesitation on his part before he released her, almost as though he was steeling himself to do so. He tethered the horses and gave them nosebags, then he unhitched the saddlebag containing their picnic lunch and handed it to Vonne.

'I'll bring the drinks and the rug,' he said. 'See if you can find a nice shady spot near the water.'

There was a patch of deep shade under a river red gum whose gnarled and twisted branches partly overhung the water where a large almost flat rock jutted into it.

'This looks perfect,' Vonne called over her shoulder to Kirk, who was striding down the slope towards her. He agreed and dumped the saddlebag containing the drinks, and the rug beside the lunch bag.

'Swim first?' he suggested, starting to peel off his shirt.

Vonne nodded. 'The water looks very inviting. It's so clear. You can see the pebbles on the bottom and there are some silvery fish darting about.'

Kirk had already shed his clothes and piled them on the rock. 'Come on,' he urged, and teasingly, 'You're not shy, are you?'

All at once she was, seeing him standing there clad only in a brief pair of trunks. Even with clothes covering it, his body had a look of muscular strength. Stripped, he was athletically lean, without an ounce of spare flesh on his broad chest, hard, flat stomach and sinewy thighs. He was deeply tanned and the sprinkling of hair on his chest was darker than on his head, almost the colour of his skin. Vonne could not help comparing him with Bart. Bart had a physique that was just as virile, she supposed, but he had affected her with nothing like the electrifying impact of this man.

She realised she was staring and hastily looked away. 'Of course I'm not!' She unbuttoned her shirt and pulled off her jeans with casual gestures, but aware all the time that he was watching her closely as her slender sun-golden body became fully revealed, except for what suddenly seemed like ludicrously inadequate strips of cloth.

'Very nice too,' murmured Kirk, with a half teasing look. 'If only the boys at the survey camp could see you now!'

Why she did it, Vonne wasn't sure, but it was probably an impulse born of sudden embarrassment as she felt the full power of his gaze on her near-naked form. In a vain effort to turn an awkward moment into horseplay in order to cover her shyness, she impulsively lunged at Kirk with the intention of pushing him into the water—a small revenge for his devastating effect on her.

But she reckoned without his surgeon's instant reflexes and his presence of mind. She also reckoned without his superior strength. He staggered only a step as she hurled herself at him, but did not overbalance. He caught her hard against him, crushing the breath out of her, and turning her blood to liquid fire with a tantalising smile that, for one instant, she thought was going to turn into a kiss. Her own lips trembled to receive it, but Kirk merely said:

'That's no way to execute a flying tackle! You'd never even make the reserve team!'

Blushing furiously, and angry with herself for such a childish display, Vonne struggled to free herself, but he held her tighter, laughing softly, and this time his mouth did claim hers with a fervour that made her heart race hectically. She made a token effort to wrest her mouth from his sweet punishment, but her resistance only made him more ardent and in fact aroused her own desires alarmingly, so she subsided limply in his arms and let the kiss happen. As soon as she gave in, he made a sudden sideways movement and plunged them both into the water.

They dived as one, lips still welded together, and as they surfaced, Vonne realised that Kirk had been in perfect control all the time. Her legs were still entwined with his, and he was supporting her. As they sank again, she wrenched her mouth away and pulled back from him. They bobbed up again, spluttering and laughing.

'Beast!' she exclaimed breathlessly.

'Witch!' he called as she swam away. Her limbs trembled almost uncontrollably as she tried to execute a masterful stroke.

'Watch out for crocs!' he yelled.

It wasn't until she was frantically scrambling out on to the nearest rock and was scanning the water in fright that she realised he had been pulling her leg. His uproarious laughter echoed across the valley. In a moment he had joined her on the rock, his eyes still full of laughter, and a lingering tenderness which caused her to experience sharp pangs in the region of her heart. It was only a small rock and he was too close for comfort. She was afraid he would kiss her again and she wouldn't have the strength to say no. So she slid back into the water and swam to the far side of the billabong where the water was in the shadow of the cliff face above. She wanted time to cool her emotions. Kirk came after her, of course, but she dodged him and swam back to the place where they had left their clothes, reaching the rock seconds ahead of him.

The sun began to dry her skin almost as soon as she climbed out of the water. She shook her wet curls and ran her fingers through them. Damp tendrils clung around her face and dried in soft wisps, giving her an attractively elfin look. She busied herself unpacking the lunch. She was perturbed by Kirk's impulsive passion, which echoed two nights ago. Perhaps it eased the hurt a little, she suddenly thought, for him to pretend she was Vicky. It wouldn't have mattered so much if she hadn't been trying not to fall in love with him herself. She wished Diana had come with them.

Kirk, in contrast to his earlier mood, seemed subdued while they ate the delicious chicken and salad and fresh bread rolls Dora had packed for them. They washed it down with iced coffee, and scarcely had they finished when Kirk scrambled up.

'What about a walk to work that lot off?' There was an odd brusqueness in his voice now that puzzled her.

'If you like.' It was probably safer to be active than lying around on the rock, Vonne thought.

She stood up and looked around. 'Where to?'

'There's a track to the top of the cliff,' said Kirk, pointing it out. 'It's not too steep, just a bit rugged in places.'

The track zigzagged up through low scrub and white-trunked gums, and proved to be a more difficult climb than Kirk had led Vonne to believe. When she paused, out of breath, at one spot where there were rocks ahead to clamber over, Kirk turned round and offered his hand. He hauled her easily over the difficult patch but did not let go of her hand, and because she felt more secure holding on to him, she did not try to pull it away. Which was just as well, because a moment or two later, she carelessly placed her foot on a loose rock and stumbled. But for Kirk's grip as she swayed perilously out over a considerable drop, she might have lost her balance, fallen, and been seriously injured.

'Steady on!' He hauled her back and they were jerked hard against each other. Vonne's heart was pounding wildly with fright and she instinctively clung to him. He held her close, his arms wrapped tightly around her with a protectiveness that was reassuring. After a moment his fingers strayed into her hair and he drew her head closer still to rest against his warm, vibrating chest.

'Don't *do* things like that to me!' he whispered hoarsely. 'You're too precious to lose.'

Vonne looked up at him. 'Oh—Kirk . . .' The shock was subsiding but her limbs were still trembling.

The lines around his mouth, that had deepened with strain, now eased into a smile that warmed his eyes as he bent his head and let his lips flutter gently over hers. 'You're so sweet—so irresistible—so damnably, in-furiatingly tantalising!' He tugged her curls, pulling her head back and covering her mouth with his. For a long moment she was plunged into the ecstasy of a kiss she wished would last for ever. Warm fingers caressed her bare back and shoulders and then moulded the soft curves of her breast against a broad palm. For blissful moments she was deceived into believing he was loving her, that what he had said was meant for her. Even if it wasn't she no longer cared. She loved him. She wasn't going to fight it any more. If she could take Vicky's place, why not do it? Why couldn't she *be* Vicky for him? There was nothing she wouldn't do for him.

Pausing for breath, he murmured, 'Don't you know that I love you, that I want you as I've never wanted a woman before?'

For a mad moment she was poised on the brink of capitulation, and the promise of ecstasy in his arms was enough to make her believe that the love in his eyes was for her. She wanted the precious moment to go on for ever and she prayed to the spirits that dwelt in this magic place to weave a spell over them . . .

Then cruel common sense crept in and prevented her giving in to the sweet temptation he offered.

Forgetting her narrow escape of only minutes before,

she pulled away from him, only one thought in her mind, to get as far away from him as possible. She began to run back the way they had come, skipping down the track, leaping rocks like a frightened wallaby, teetering precariously in places, nearly falling once or twice, prevented from doing so only by her own crazy momentum. Miraculously she reached the spot where they had picnicked without mishap. She stopped, breathless and trembling, her chest aching from the effort of running, and the emotion she felt. The justification for her flight still rang in her ears. As she had fled, Kirk had involuntarily cried out, 'Vicky, stop! You'll kill yourself!' Vicky, he'd called out, not Vonne, realising her worst fears, smashing her foolish dreams.

Kirk reached her side seconds later and caught her angrily by the arm. There was no passion now, no tenderness either.

'You little fool! You could have fallen! Wasn't one narrow escape enough?'

Vonne could not bear to look at him. She'd just had a narrow escape, she thought, that he wasn't even thinking about. How could she have been so foolish as to think she could take Vicky's place? He would break her heart in the end even more cruelly than Leith had done. He wasn't even aware, she realised, that he had called Vicky's name in the moment of panic, but it was all she needed to prove that his mind and emotions were still centred on her sister, and that she was only a visual focus for his feelings.

'Kirk, let me go!' She tried to twist away from him, but his grip tightened and his eyes flashed angrily as though he'd caught her in a criminal act. Then abruptly his mood changed.

'I'm sorry—I'd almost begun to think . . .' He forced her to face him, but his grip had relaxed and his voice was surprisingly full of concern. 'You told me you'd been jilted. Are you afraid . . .'

'Kirk, don't, please!' she begged.

'Do you still hope . . . ?'

She shook her head wildly. 'No! No, I don't. It's all over.'

'Why did you run from me?' His eyes darkened and there was an edge to his voice. 'Is there someone else now? Is it Bart?' He spoke the name half angrily, half derisively.

The urge to tell him that she loved him almost overwhelmed her, but she resisted it. The illusion that she and Vicky were somehow one and the same person would eventually wear off and he would hate himself for having pretended to love her.

There was only one way out at that moment. 'If you must know, yes, it is!' she said in desperation.

Kirk was incredulous. 'But he's only fooling around.' He dropped her arm as though she had suddenly become tainted. 'You know he's married?'

'Yes, I know.'

'Are you quite mad? He'll . . .'

'Kirk, it's none of your business,' she cut across him sharply. 'I don't want to discuss it.' She was wishing now that she hadn't let him trap her into this monstrous lie. What if he said something to Bart? She begged urgently, 'Please—you won't say anything to him, will you?'

He shook his head wonderingly from side to side. 'I really thought you'd have had more sense . . .' He did not promise but stooped to pack up the picnic things. 'You're a very silly little girl,' he said contemptuously, and Vonne felt that indeed she must be.

CHAPTER TEN

AFTER the weekend at Walparoo, Vonne was more thankful than ever that she was working on the men's wards. Seeing Kirk was becoming more and more painful, and dismally she faced the fact that her feelings had deepened, not diminished, during those two days. Somehow she had to stop her love from growing, but how? Not being in daily contact with him did not really help. He filled her thoughts day and night. Lying in bed in her flat, she would feel his arms around her again and give herself up to the remembered magic of his kiss. She would pretend that he had never met Vicky and that it was she, Vonne, whom he truly loved.

'You're looking a bit under the weather,' Kelly remarked one day when they were having lunch together in the canteen, for the first time in quite a while. 'Who's been keeping you out late at night?'

Vonne forced herself to be cheery. 'No one! Well, not very late very often.'

'How's Bart?' asked Kelly, cautiously.

'He's OK.' Vonne did not want to tell Kelly that Bart had been uncharacteristically distant and preoccupied since he had come back from his holiday. He had told her nothing about where he had been and she had not liked to ask, but she suspected that something rather disturbing had happened.

'I hope you're not losing your heart to him,' Kelly said bluntly. 'I mean, he's very attractive and all that, but men like Bart Webb never settle down. They're always off to new pastures and new conquests. You'd have done better to set your cap at Kirk Leveson.'

154

Vonne's heart quickened involuntarily at the mention of his name. She had not seen Kirk for a couple of weeks, except in the distance, and even though she longed to be with him if only for a minute or two, she had always evaporated as promptly as possible.

Kelly pulled a face. 'It's a bit late now, though. Lorin's turning the screw as hard as she dares. They've been seen out together a few times lately and I heard that he's teaching her to play golf.'

The news hurt, but it was inevitable, she supposed. She hated the picture of them together that immediately invaded her mind. If Kirk eventually married Lorin, as he probably would, at least it would be easier for him to love her for herself, not just because she was a living reminder of a lost love.

'Hey, dreamer, are you going to eat your custard tart or not?' Kelly's demand broke Vonne's daydream. 'If not, I will!'

'You can have it, I'm not hungry,' said Vonne, pushing the plate of dessert towards her friend.

'You really are below par,' remarked Kelly with concern. 'Are they working you down to the shins in Men's Surgical?'

'We're busy,' conceded Vonne, 'but it's not all that hectic. I'm just a bit tired from all my other activities, I suppose. I've had a few late nights recently. I've been helping with first aid classes for the Youth Club one night a week. That's a bit riotous!'

Kelly grimaced. 'You bet it is! I did it for a few months once.' She chuckled reminiscently. 'I'll never forget the night they did a bandage job on me and trussed me up with every bandaging technique in the book. I couldn't move an inch and the only bit of me not covered was my eyes and nose. They said they were going to ring the Museum and say they'd found a mummy!'

'What happened?' Vonne asked through laughter.

'They relented in the end and untied me. We had a

good laugh and I felt obliged to give them all proficiency certificates!'

Vonne always felt cheered when she had talked to Kelly and had heard all the gossip from the women's wards. She did not admit to herself that her interest was largely in case Kelly dropped any snippet about Kirk, but apart from what she had already said, today Kelly had nothing to tell.

Diana had insisted that Vonne should keep in touch, and Vonne tried to keep this promise in a guarded kind of way. Diana, she was sure, had never suspected that anything untoward had occurred between her and Kirk that Sunday at Walparoo. They had both managed to maintain a friendly if slightly constrained atmosphere for the remainder of the weekend. Vonne dropped into the pharmacy in town now and then for a chat with Diana, and occasionally went to Seaford Street to tea. Each time she wasn't sure whether she hoped or feared that Kirk would be there too. He never was, and she was always torn between relief and bitter disappointment.

The last time Diana had been more than disappointed. She had been perplexed, and had said bluntly, 'I thought you and Kirk were getting along very well, especially that weekend at Walparoo, but when I asked if you were coming with us again last week, he said you were on duty. Were you? Or have you quarrelled?' she finished pointedly.

Vonne didn't know how to answer Diana's forthrightness without giving too much away. 'No,' she said carefully, 'not exactly.'

Diana's expression was thoughtful. 'I know it's none of my business, but I am a bit of a busybody where people I'm fond of are concerned, and when I asked him that question he just shrugged and said something vague about not trespassing on other people's property.'

Vonne did not want to perpetuate the lie about Bart, so she said, 'I imagine that was just an excuse. I'm quite sure Kirk has other female interests.'

'Not Lorin Kent again, I hope,' said Diana with feeling.

'Why not? She's very attractive. And they've known each other for quite a while, I believe. Wasn't he going about with her before he met Vicky?'

'Don't stick up for her!' protested Diana. 'I know all about the way she treated you. She's a possessive, jealous woman and I'd be astonished if Kirk really can't see through her.'

'She may be quite a different person with him,' Vonne said.

Diana pursed her lips disdainfully. 'Well, what he does is his affair. I've never tried to manipulate my children—well, not much! I suppose if he does decide to marry her, I'll have to try and like the girl.' She sighed with resignation.

A few weeks later Vonne was asked if she would do a night shift on the Maternity Wards. She almost said flatly, no, because she was bound to see Kirk too often for comfort, but she could think of no plausible excuse that wasn't the truth, and she dared not confess that. So she had to comply.

She expected Bart to express disappointment that she wouldn't be available for dates in the evenings so often, but he wasn't.

He said, 'Maybe it's just as well,' and with a rather wistful smile went on, 'I'm a bit too fond of you, Vonne. I could be very jealous of the guy who wins your heart.'

'I doubt if I'll ever get married,' Vonne said soberly.

He scoffed at that. 'Rubbish! You, as a crabbed old Director of Nursing? Never! You'll get married, my dear, and raise a family just like I did, only you'll be a lot more conscientious about it than I was. I left it all to Marcia. It's no wonder she left me.' A sober look replaced his cheerful expression. 'Do you want to know where I went for the holiday I took a while back?'

'You were so cagey about it, I didn't like to pry.'

'Well, I went to Sydney. I saw Marcia, and we had a long talk. She's not living with Trevor any more. I think she might have me back if I tried to reform.'

'Bart!'

'I was in the wrong,' he said, as though glad to talk about it. 'I was a selfish beast. I guess we married too young, and I hadn't sowed enough wild oats.' He grimaced ruefully. 'I can't help how I am, not altogether, but I've been thinking a lot over these past weeks, and I owe it to my girls to give it another try.'

'Bart, that's wonderful,' Vonne said warmly, but added anxiously, 'Will Marcia have you back?'

He grinned. 'More fool her, I suppose you'd say. But I think so. I wrote a week or two ago and told her I'd been thinking it over, and I got an answer today.' He drew a thick envelope out of his pocket and waved it in her face. 'A lot of conditions!'

'But she still loves you.'

'I reckon she must—a bit.' His old carefree manner reasserted itself. 'Or else she's got a lot of invitations to dinner and balls and can't find a respectable partner!'

'Bart, you're incorrigible!' exclaimed Vonne. 'I'm sure she still loves you. You're a bit of a rake, but you're a very lovable man!'

'Now you tell me!'

'It's only now I dare to! Go home and stay faithful. The girls need you, and so, I'm sure, does Marcia. I bet they've missed you terribly.'

He sighed. 'If only they knew how much I've missed them!'

A week later he had gone. At first Vonne missed his cheery voice on the telephone inviting her out to dinner or a weekend drive, his sudden appearance on the wards, breathing down her neck and sliding his hands around her waist as he teased her flatteringly. But she had known it would have to end, one way or another. Even if Bart hadn't been married already, she would never have fallen in love with him. There was only one man she would ever love now.

The day after Bart went south, back to his family, Kirk appeared one evening, for the first time since Vonne had been on nights. He had performed an emergency Caesarian only a short time before and had come down to the ward to check on the patient. The baby had been stillborn.

Mrs Barber was in a single room and Vonne and one of the other nurses, Jill, had just finished making her comfortable when Kirk arrived. He looked rather drawn. The patient was calm but tearful, and as soon as Kirk sat on the edge of the bed she clutched his hand tightly and her tears flowed unchecked. He began talking to her in a low soothing voice, and it was as though, Vonne thought, he actually shared her sorrow. A lump came into her throat as she looked at the work-weary face of the man who never stopped until he had done everything he could for a patient. She loved him so painfully at that moment she was afraid it would shine out of her like a neon sign.

Struggling for composure, she followed Jill quietly out of the room.

'She fell, didn't she?' said Jill, her young pretty face crumpling with sympathy. 'It must be terrible to lose your baby like that. I suppose you could be forgiven for thinking the doctors didn't try hard enough to save it.'

'I'm sure Dr Leveson did everything in his power,' Vonne said with conviction, 'but I know what you mean.'

'I wonder if he'll ever get married,' reflected Jill ingenuously. 'I thought he was keen on Lorin Kent, but the other day I heard a rumour that she's been seen drooling over engagement rings with Dr Terson—you know, that good-looking radiologist who's only been up here a few weeks. She's a fast worker all right! I wonder what happened between her and Dr Leveson.'

Vonne was astonished by this piece of gossip and had a hard job not showing it. First she experienced a feeling of relief that Kirk was not going to marry Lorin after all, and then she was sorry for him because Lorin had found someone else. Or was it he who had broken off their relationship because he was still bedevilled by Vicky? That was probably it. Lorin, surely, would never have broken it off.

She declined to comment on the news, however, saying, 'Don't you think it's about time you did your obs, Jill?'

'I'm on my way,' said Jill, and dashed off with her usual alacrity.

Vonne went back to the nurses' station and tried to concentrate on paperwork, but her thoughts kept straying to the man in room two with Mrs Barber. She was still writing busily when she sensed a presence near her and looked up. Kirk was standing on the other side of the desk. There was a preoccupied expression in his eyes and the signs of recent strain were still clearly etched in his face. Vonne wanted to reach up and soothe them away with a longing that was almost unbearable.

'How is she?' she asked, and half rising from her chair, 'Is there anything you want me to . . . ?'

'No. She's asleep now,' he said. 'The sedative will probably keep her that way until morning. Call me at once if there's any problem. She suffered rather severe depression during her pregnancy and having it terminated like this has been a heavy blow. The trouble is she won't be able to have any more children.'

'Has she any?'

'A girl, aged three. They were hoping for a boy. Her husband is a long-distance lorry driver. A relative is getting in touch with him, but it'll be two days at least before he gets back. She's going to suffer in the meantime—she's afraid he'll blame her for being careless, that sort of thing.'

'How did the fall happen?'

'She was hanging up some curtains that had just been dry-cleaned. It wasn't a heavy fall, just bad luck. That's how it goes sometimes.' Kirk heaved a weary sigh. 'The baby probably died instantly.'

'I suppose you'd like her specialled for a day or two?' Vonne suggested.

'Yes, please. She may want to talk to someone quite often.'

'I'll put it in the report.' Vonne made a note on her pad.

She expected him to go, but he perched on the edge of the desk and stayed, as though he too needed company or reassurance. He raked his fingers absently through his hair.

Vonne asked, 'Would you like a cup of coffee—or tea? I can soon make one.'

A grateful smile curved his lips. 'Would you? I'd love a cup of tea.'

He was still hunched on the corner of her desk, arms folded, brooding, when she came back with the tea and biscuits.

'Why don't you take a chair?' she suggested gently. 'You'd be more comfortable.'

He seemed startled at her voice as though unaware for a moment where he was. His weariness was even more pronounced. He's been overworking, Vonne thought —or perhaps he is upset about Lorin after all. She wished she could soothe him as he had soothed Mrs Barber—only she wanted to hold him in her arms to comfort him with love as well as compassion. But all she could do was offer biscuits.

'End of packet,' she apologised, 'mostly crumbs, I'm afraid.'

His fingers brushed hers as she handed him the mug of

tea, and she averted her eyes, unwilling to let his gaze disconcert her even more than she already was.

'How's your mother?' she asked, after a lengthy silence, and choosing what she hoped was a safe topic for them both.

'She's fine—very well,' he answered. She could see he was forcing himself to make conversation, so she didn't try again. Just let him unwind, she thought, and went back to her reports, pretending to concentrate on them when that was the last thing she felt capable of doing.

Finally he startled her by speaking. 'I'm sorry, Vonne.'

She glanced up, perplexed. 'Sorry? Whatever for?'

'Bart—it must have been a blow for you. But it was bound to happen.'

She remembered his scorn that day at the billabong when she had allowed him to think she was in love with Bart. She must choose her words carefully now, she realised, if she wasn't to give herself away.

She said, 'I hope he makes a go of it this time. I rather think he will.'

Kirk's eyes met hers and she couldn't drag hers away. 'It's always a mistake to fall in love with someone you know you can't have,' he said slowly. He probably thought she was being brave.

Vonne searched for something to say, but was saved by the appearance of Jill, who said, 'Sorry to butt in—I just wanted to ask . . .' She glanced apologetically at Kirk.

'Don't mind me,' said Kirk, rising. He put his empty mug down on the desk. 'I'm just going.' His eyes lingered for a moment on Vonne's face as he said, 'Thanks for the tea.' Then he turned abruptly away and with his hands stuffed deep in his pockets, departed.

'Gee,' said Jill on a long-drawn-out sigh, 'he's gorgeous, isn't he?'

'Yes, he's very nice,' agreed Vonne, which must have

been the biggest understatement of her life.

Not surprisingly, Vonne was unable to sleep when she returned home at the end of her shift. She tossed and turned for an hour or two, but the power-mowers racketing up and down the hospital lawns were noisily intrusive. Eventually she got up and decided to go into the city.

How many more months before my contract is up? she thought, and calculated it. She had been at the Bauhinia over four months now. It would soon be Christmas. Her first Christmas away from England. What would Vicky be doing? she wondered. She would be away from England too, celebrating the festival in France with Armand. Suddenly Vonne felt a pang of envy for her sister, and yet she still had an underlying feeling of unease. She hadn't heard from Vicky for quite a while, that was the trouble.

In town she browsed around the shops and in a fit of extravagance bought herself a new outfit, a smart blue linen two-piece with a blue and white spotted blouse. While she was in the shop trying it on, there was a sudden storm and when she came out the streets were awash, although the sun was already coming out.

It was very humid, and she decided that what she needed was a nice long cold drink and a light lunch. She was about to make her way to the coffee shop of one of the hotels, when an ambulance siren caused her to turn automatically. She saw it screaming over the intersection behind her, racing to an accident, she guessed, probably a crash caused by the sudden storm making the roads slippery.

As she turned quickly to continue on the way she was going, she collided with a pedestrian coming towards her.

'Vonne!'

It was Kirk. 'Oh—I'm sorry—not looking where I was going . . .' She was caught off guard and she couldn't think of anything sensible to say, and besides, he was looking at her in the oddest way, almost as if he didn't recognise her.

'Where are you going?' he asked. 'I thought all good night nurses were still fast asleep at this time.'

'I—I wanted to do some shopping.' She was fumbling with words like a student nurse fumbling with sheets on her first bedmaking task. 'And now I'm going to have some lunch. I heard an ambulance . . .' It all sounded very irrelevant.

'I was just going to have a bite myself,' said Kirk. He looked less weary than last night, she noticed, and was glad. 'Why don't we go together?' he suggested, and caught hold of her arm as though determined not to let her get away. 'Come on. I know a nice quiet place where they do the most exotic salads you've ever eaten!'

She was too bemused to invent an excuse, so she let him take her to the place he recommended. It was not crowded and the display of food was lavish and on a help-yourself basis. Suddenly, however, Vonne did not feel hungry any more. Nevertheless, at Kirk's insistence, she filled her plate, and by the time they sat down in a quiet corner, her appetite had returned and she was able to do decent justice to the food.

They talked intermittently, about Mrs Barber and the baby that had died, about the Wet, about a whole lot of things, and an hour sped by on wings. Since Vonne had nothing particular to make her hurry off, and neither, it seemed, had Kirk, they lingered over several cups of coffee, still talking even after most of the lunchtime diners had gone. No one seemed to mind, and a waitress was happy to keep refilling their cups.

Finally Kirk looked at his watch. 'I'll have to go soon.'

Vonne was astonished at how late it was. 'Me too! I'm sorry—I didn't realise . . .' She felt guilty for detaining him.

'Don't apologise. It's been very pleasant,' he said

smilingly, and after a moment added, 'I wonder if you'd care to come to Walparoo again the next time I go, in a couple of weeks' time. People asked after you the last time.'

Vonne was again caught off guard. She knew it would be wisest to refuse, but somehow the words wouldn't come. She was remembering that day at the billabong, what he had said, why she had run away from him, and how she had deceived him over Bart, but it made no difference—she wanted to go . . .

And if she went, she knew, she would be accepting what he had obliquely offered that day—a love that wasn't quite hers, a love that belonged to Vicky. But if she was patient, couldn't it perhaps one day belong to her? The temptation was suddenly too great to resist. She loved him too much not to take the risk. He was looking at her expectantly.

'I'd like to,' she said, and the relief in his eyes warmed her. She knew he had asked her because Bart was now out of her life, and she knew he would treat her very gently for a while because he believed she had been hurt by Bart.

Afterwards she did not allow herself to dwell on the recklessness of her decision. It was made, and that was that. She had realised that unless her life was bound up with Kirk's, it would be a bleak existence. Being with him on any terms at all was preferable to not.

Diana did not come that weekend. It was a deliberate ploy, Vonne felt certain, to give them a chance to be completely alone. It was a blissful weekend. Vonne helped Kirk with the surgery as she had on the previous occasion, and on Sunday they did nothing but loaf around the homestead.

Although the skies were clear, there had been storms and it was too wet to ride. Kirk had suggested a flight over Katherine Gorge, which he said was a spectacular sight in full spate, as it was then, but the weather forecast was unfavourable, so they did not chance it. Vonne was perfectly happy just to be with him, talking or just companionably silent. And he seemed happy and relaxed too.

There was no passion in their relationship that weekend. When Kirk kissed her good night, it was with tenderness and concern, although she could sense his iron control. She knew he was trying not to force himself on her out of respect for her feelings, as he believed, for Bart. Although she ached to be in his arms in a more passionate embrace, she did not attempt to change the mood. It was as though they were making a new start.

Resolutely, she put all thoughts of Vicky from her mind, and allowed herself to believe that it was not because she resembled her sister that Kirk wanted her, but for herself. It was a masterpiece of self-delusion, she knew, but one that given sufficient time and patience, might become reality. She would make it come true, she vowed. And meanwhile, if her being a substitute for Vicky made Kirk happy, she was happy to play the role.

At Sunday lunch the subject of Christmas arose and Kirk said, 'We usually come here for Christmas. If you're not rostered, Mother and I would like you to come too, Vonne.' There was a wealth of meaning in the smile he gave her, and Vonne's heart leapt.

'I'd love to,' she said. 'But I won't know until the new rosters are posted what my shifts will be for December. But thank you, anyway.'

'I can always come and get you if it doesn't quite fit in,' he offered. 'You're bound to have at least one day off. Besides,' he added with a grin, 'there's no guarantee I'll be able to spend the whole holiday here myself. Babies get born and emergencies happen regardless of holidays. I shall be on call, in any case, for part of the time. But we'll work something out.'

Vonne was in a very relaxed and happy frame of mind when they flew back to Darwin on Sunday evening.

Everything had changed suddenly, without fuss, without drama, in a comfortable and wonderfully reassuring way. Kirk had said nothing about a steady relationship between them, but Vonne knew that was what he wanted. It might not be perfect, she thought, but perfection is too much to expect of life.

There was just one worry overriding all others now, and that was Vicky. Vonne still hadn't heard. All weekend she had been dying to confide her anxiety in Kirk, but she had vowed never to mention Vicky's name unless he did. She would never remind him of her sister if she could help it, not until she was sure he had got over her. It would be difficult. When two people were as close as she and her twin, it was difficult for one not to talk about the other, sometimes.

Almost as though her worrying had communicated itself to Vicky, there was a letter in the post the day after Vonne returned from the weekend at Walparoo. It was the first in nearly two months, and Vonne tore open the flimsy blue airmail form, anxious for reassurance. Her eyes skimmed over Vicky's wayward writing that wandered in slanting lines down the page, to discover if there was anything wrong, if perhaps she had been ill.

'Oh, no!' she exclaimed, as the words leapt out of the page at her. 'Oh, Vicky—no!'

White-faced, she read it through again more slowly, making sure there was no misunderstanding. There wasn't. It was terribly clear. Vicky had not beaten about the bush, and as usual she had underlined a lot of words.

'. . . so Armand and I have *parted*. It was a *crazy* affair, Vonne, and couldn't last. I suppose I knew that, but I was *infatuated* with him and I think he was with me, for a time. Well, I won't bore you with the sordid details, they can wait till we meet, and here's the crunch, love. *Please*, can I come and stay with you for a while—over Christmas particularly? I feel a bit shattered, and I want to get far far away. Do say I can come and I'll be on the next flight. I'm *longing* to see you. Please phone me at Sylvia's if it's all right.'

The ending was typically Vicky. 'I can hardly wait to see you, Vonne. It's been such *ages*. I've missed you *terribly*!'

Vonne read the letter through several times more, still not quite believing it.

'Oh, Vicky,' she murmured helplessly.

She would tell her to come, of course. What else could she do? She would borrow a folding bed and put her up for a few days at least. Vicky had said nothing of what she wanted to do, how long she wanted to stay.

Reluctantly, Vonne forced herself to think of how it would affect her and Kirk. What would happen when he and Vicky met again, as they were bound to? She hardly dared think about it. Would seeing Kirk re-inflame Vicky's feelings for him?

She thought of her own tenuous grasp on happiness, and the hope she had been nurturing that in time Kirk would love her for herself, not because she resembled her sister. She could of course prevent Kirk from seeing her sister. She could tell Vicky not to come. The temptation was strong and she paced the floor many times arguing with herself over it. But in the end she knew she could not put her own selfish needs ahead of his or her sister's.

So she called Sylvia's number, and with a bleak heart waited for someone to answer.

CHAPTER ELEVEN

DURING the next few days, Vonne's feelings about Vicky's arrival were in constant conflict. She was thrilled at the prospect of seeing her sister again, but also filled with apprehension.

She borrowed a fold-up bed from Kelly's family and spent a whole afternoon rearranging the furniture in the bedsitting-room to try to make it look as little cluttered as possible.

Fortunately, she was able to juggle her shifts so that she was able to meet Vicky's plane from Singapore, which would be arriving in the early hours of the morning. She had said nothing to anyone except Kelly about Vicky's imminent arrival as she did not want Kirk to know—not yet. Not before she had talked to Vicky herself.

Strictly speaking, visitors were not allowed to stay in the nurses' quarters, but when Vonne asked if she could put her sister up for a few days until she found other suitable accommodation, Sister Howard had given permission. She was deputising for John Langham who was away for a couple of weeks' holiday, a fact which Vonne was rather glad about. The DN just might have told Kirk about Vicky's coming. At the very least he would have been curious.

'So long as it's only for a few days,' Sister Howard stipulated. 'I don't think Mr Langham would approve if you all started making a habit of it. You know what it could lead to—not just sisters!'

When Vonne saw Vicky at the airport she was shocked—her sister was so pale and thin, and looked so unhappy. She had never seen her looking so wan and defeated before. On the telephone she had sounded as ebullient as ever, but now Vonne saw that it had been bravado. Vicky looked weary and despairing. She was bound to be suffering from jet-lag, despite the stopover in Singapore, but her appearance spoke of more than mere travel-weariness.

'Vicky!' Vonne shouted excitedly as soon as she spotted her.

'Vonne!' A glimpse of Vicky's old spirit broke through in her smile.

They embraced warmly and Vicky said, tears in her eyes, 'Oh, Vonne, it's so good to see you. So good to be here.'

Vonne hugged her spontaneously again. 'And it's marvellous to see you.'

Vicky pulled a face. 'What an unearthly hour to arrive!'

Vonne laughed. 'When I came here my flight was delayed and it was nearer to breakfast-time when I arrived. I didn't get any breakfast though, because of the accident—remember I told you about that?'

'Yes. I thought it was hilarious. On your first day too. I could just imagine it!' But Vicky was not laughing now. 'How's Kirk?' There was an abrupt urgency to her question, and Vonne guessed he had been on her mind all the way.

Vonne looked sharply into her face, searching for a clue as to her feelings, but the features that so accurately mirrored her own showed only strain and tiredness.

'He's fine,' said Vonne, and because she didn't quite trust herself to speak noncommittally about him, hurried on, 'I've got the whole day off, so we'll have plenty of time to talk. But first, I expect you'll want to have a good sleep.'

'I haven't slept properly for weeks,' Vicky confessed. Tears filled her eyes. 'Oh, it was awful, Vonne, really rotten awful. I made a terrible fool of myself over

Armand. He had all these other women . . .'

There was no stemming the flood once she had started. She talked all the way to the car and on the way to Vonne's flat, and Vonne let her, feeling it could only help to get Armand out of her system.

'He kept talking about getting married,' Vicky said miserably, 'and at first I thought it was, as he'd said, just a matter of time before his family got used to the idea. They were pleasant to me, but very aloof, and I could see that his *maman* wasn't altogether thrilled at the idea of his marrying an English girl. She had no need to worry—he never intended to. I was just a challenge, a novelty.'

'Did he live with you?' Vonne asked tentatively.

'No. I had this super little flat attached to the clinic, which I paid for myself out of my salary.' She gave Vonne a twisted little smile. 'I always was independent! We both are, aren't we?' She went on wistfully, 'At first it was wonderful. I loved Paris and Armand took me everywhere, and he had such interesting friends. I was on top of the world. But I wasn't amorous enough for him—I didn't want an affair, and he soon grew tired of waiting for me to be subdued by his charms. I discovered he was seeing a girl called Françoise, a doctor at the clinic, and worse, Vonne, much worse . . .' Her voice faltered.

'What?'

'He already had a daughter by a girl in Lyons—he used to work in a clinic there. He was, to put it generously, a bit of a rake. And I fell for it . . .' She leaned back and closed her eyes, her face a picture of self-disgust.

'But you were in love with him,' Vonne excused.

Vicky's eyes flipped open and flashed angrily. 'No, I wasn't! I could kick myself for being such a fool. I was just infatuated with him, with his Gallic charm, his glamour—no, I wasn't in love with him, Vonne. And in a way that makes it worse. I feel so cheap, so foolish . . .'

She sighed deeply. 'I couldn't bear staying in France, so I went straight back to England and Sylvia took me in. But I couldn't bear it there either, knowing what a fool they must think me. Sylvia had said in the first place that I was crazy to give up Kirk for Armand, and she was right. You were right too. I was so stupid . . .'

'Here we are,' Vonne interrupted as they came up to the hospital's main entrance and turned into the parking area beside the nurses' quarters.

'My flat's on the top floor.'

Vicky gathered up her belongings and Vonne carried her suitcase up. Inside the tiny apartment, Vicky looked around approvingly.

'It's nice,' she said, somewhat wistfully.

'Do you want to go straight to bed?' asked Vonne. 'Or would you like some breakfast first? It's not too early?'

Vicky said, 'I wouldn't mind a cup of coffee, but I'm not hungry.'

She sank down on to Vonne's settee and leaned back, staring dismally at the ceiling. When Vonne returned with coffee, she was fast asleep. Vonne shifted her so that her head rested on a pillow and her feet were propped up on the arm of the couch. Vicky did not stir.

Vonne had breakfast alone and tried not to contemplate the likely consequence of her twin's appearance in Darwin. She was almost resigned to the inevitable.

Presently, wanting to leave Vicky to sleep undisturbed, Vonne took her laundry down to the ground floor utility room where the communal washing-machine, drier and irons were housed. By the time she had finished her washing and ironing, the shops were open, so she drove down to the nearest supermarket for a few odds and ends, more out of a desire to fill in time than because she really needed anything. She had already stocked up her cupboards and the refrigerator to cater for her guest.

It was ten o'clock when she let herself quietly back

into the flat and tiptoed to the kitchen. It was quite likely, she thought, that Vicky would sleep the clock round. However, a few minutes later, Vicky stirred and called out, 'Vonne?'

'Sorry. Did I disturb you?' Vonne went over to the couch.

'No . . .'

'Are you feeling better? You've had a few hours' sleep. It might be best not to sleep too much during the day, then you'll sleep normally tonight. Otherwise your biological clock will stay out of gear.'

Vicky sat up. 'I feel ghastly—like a hangover. Can I have a shower?'

'Yes, of course—go right ahead. There are towels in the bathroom for you, the blue ones. I'll put the coffee on again and if you're feeling peckish we'll have brunch.'

Half an hour later, Vicky reappeared, looking much refreshed. She had changed into slinky green pants and a form-fitting white cotton top, both of which had a chic Frenchness about them, Vonne thought.

'Phew! That's better,' said Vicky, as she joined Vonne in the kitchen. 'I felt like death warmed up this morning when I arrived!' She gave her sister an affectionate kiss on the cheek. 'Thanks for meeting me, love, and thanks most of all for *having* me!'

Vonne responded with a quick hug. 'It's terrific having you here.'

Vicky sighed. 'Just the way it should have been . . .' She gave Vonne a sharp look. 'Kirk—he's not married or anything?'

Vonne felt shaky inside. 'He would hardly have got over you that quickly,' she said.

'No . . .' Vicky said thoughtfully. 'Perhaps not.' She perched on a stool at the breakfast bar that divided the kitchen from the bedsitting-room, and sipped the coffee Vonne pushed across to her.

'Would you like some sandwiches?' asked Vonne.

Vicky nodded absently, and after a pause, asked plaintively, 'Vonne, was he very angry with me?'

'And hurt.' Vonne's own anger at the way her sister had treated Kirk surfaced involuntarily.

'But you explained?'

'I did the best I could.'

'Do you think he's forgiven me?' Vicky asked, her eyes desperately hopeful.

Vonne cut savagely through the pile of sandwiches she was making. 'Vicky, Kirk is a very private man. You should know that. How should I know how he feels?' But I do, she thought, I do, and it's tearing me apart. If she wasn't careful, she realised, she could end up quarrelling with her sister.

Vicky's contrite expression softened her reaction. 'I was so naïve—such a stupid fool, Vonne,' she wailed. 'I don't know why I couldn't see . . .' She appealed for understanding with wide brown eyes which Vonne knew Kirk would be bound to find irresistible. 'Did you tell him I was coming?' This last, eagerly.

Vonne shook her head. 'I thought it best not to say anything to anybody until I'd talked to you.' She wasn't sure whether Vicky was relieved or disappointed.

Vicky slid off the stool, and with her coffee in one hand, a sandwich in the other, prowled around the living-room. After a few moments, she paused and turned to Vonne to ask bluntly, 'Do you think he'd have me back?' Her voice trembled on the words.

'He might,' Vonne answered cautiously. 'I'm not Kirk's confidante, Vicky. You'll have to ask him yourself.'

If only Vicky hadn't been foolish over Armand, she was thinking, none of this would be taking place. She, Vonne, wouldn't have fallen in love with Kirk, and there wouldn't be a pain in her heart now that was almost beyond bearing.

Vicky paced up and down again. 'I'm scared!'

'He may not forgive you lightly,' Vonne said slowly. 'He'll have every right to be wary, even if he still loves you. You hurt him deeply.'

'But do *you* think he still loves me?' Vicky persisted.

Vonne was torn between wanting to reassure her sister and wanting to protect Kirk. 'The point is, do you love him? Maybe you only think you do because it all went wrong with Armand.' She added passionately, 'Don't hurt him again!'

Vicky looked at her sharply. 'You haven't fallen in love with him yourself, have you?' she asked.

'No, of course not! I hardly ever see him.' It wasn't true and said a little too promptly. It would be hard to fool Vicky, Vonne thought. They had always been very intuitive about each other.

Vicky considered her doubtfully for a moment, then said, 'I hope you mean that, Vonne. I wouldn't want you to be hurt again, not after Leith . . .'

'No way,' said Vonne bravely. 'Look, Vicky, I like and admire Kirk, and I don't think he deserves to be trifled with. I just hope that before you try to turn the clock back and take up where you left off, you're absolutely sure of yourself this time.' She emphasised, 'Are you?'

Vicky turned away and stared out of the window across the green lawns towards the hospital, where Kirk, thought Vonne, was very likely at this moment operating or visiting a patient, totally unaware that destiny waited only a hundred metres away.

It was only when she noticed her sister's shoulders shaking that Vonne realised she was crying. She went to her at once and put an arm around her, not speaking. Words had never been necessary for them to comfort each other.

At last Vicky dashed the tears away and sniffed, searching for a handkerchief. She found one and blew her nose, then said sheepishly, 'Sorry about that. I just don't know where I am, who I am, where I'm going or what I want at the moment. I've made an unholy mess of my life. I desperately want to pick up the pieces. I *think* I still love Kirk—but I have to see him. I have to know if he . . .' She broke off helplessly.

'Shall I tell him you're here?' offered Vonne.

Vicky looked terrified. 'No—no, he might refuse to see me. You said he was angry. He—he might not know how he feels until he actually sees me again.' She paused, then added tentatively, 'If we could just bump into each other . . .'

Vonne shook her head. 'That might be difficult to arrange. Why don't you just call him, or go round to his house?'

'I—I couldn't, said Vicky. 'He might hang up on me—or he might have someone else at his house.'

Vonne began to feel a little impatient with her. If she wanted to effect a reconciliation with Kirk, then it was up to her to plunge in and hope for the best. Vonne had few doubts about how it would turn out in the end, but nevertheless she appreciated Vicky's difficulty in plucking up the courage to approach the man she had jilted.

'You could hang around the hospital on the offchance of seeing him,' she suggested, 'or go to his surgery.'

Vicky shook her head. 'No—no, I couldn't.'

Vonne knew what she was leading up to. She wanted her to act as mediator. Just as she had used her sister to break the news to him that she had gone off with another man, she now wanted her to soften him up with a view to reconciliation.

No, Vonne thought angrily, I can't do it. Not loving him too.

She refilled their coffee cups. 'Please, Vicky,' she advised, 'let's sleep on it. You're a bit uptight at the moment after the flight and everything. Don't worry, we'll work something out. Meanwhile, how about a drive around Darwin and then a meal somewhere? I'm not on duty until ten.'

Vicky capitulated. 'You're right—there's no need to rush into it. That's the trouble with me, Vonne, I do rush into things. You're much more cautious and sensible.' She smiled affectionately, and Vonne ceased to be angry with her.

'I'm not always,' she said.

They did not mention Kirk again all afternoon, although Vonne knew he must be in the forefront of her sister's mind just as he was in her own.

Vonne drove Vicky to see all the most interesting sights of Darwin and ended up with a trip to East Point, although it was too early for sunset. Vicky seemed genuinely interested in everything, and Vonne did not dare remind her how she had scoffed at the notion of living so far from England. She wondered how Vicky would take to Walparoo.

Over dinner, which they had in a quiet little place Bart had sometimes taken Vonne to, Vicky talked about Armand again, and her life in Paris, but without so much emotion now, and even sometimes with humour. She questioned Vonne closely about life in Darwin, and the hospital, and seemed anxious to appear interested. But what she most wanted to hear about was Kirk.

Vonne told her about Lorin and to her surprise Vicky said, 'Yes, he told me about her! He would never have married her, though. He said she was a leech! I think he went to England to get away from her when she was getting too possessive. He said she was beautiful but cold.'

'She is,' Vonne agreed. She was relieved that Kirk had probably never really been serious about Lorin.

So too, apparently, was Vicky. 'I'm glad he didn't fall into her arms on the rebound!' she said. 'What a disaster that would have been!'

Eventually Vonne said, 'I'll have to be going soon, Vicky.'

Vicky yawned. 'I don't mind. I'm about ready for bed.'

Vonne waved the waiter who was hovering with the coffee pot away and asked for the bill. She was automatically checking the addition when she felt a presence at the table and glanced up.

'Kirk!' Her shock was profound. She glanced anxiously at Vicky and saw her sister's face go white, her mouth fall half open. Vicky's eyes were wide with shock and apprehension.

Kirk's gaze snapped swiftly from one to the other and his brow creased in a puzzled frown.

'Vicky . . .' he muttered incredulously. 'Where have you sprung from?'

'I flew in this morning,' Vicky managed to croak.

'A surprise?' he queried, with a quizzical look at Vonne.

'No,' she was forced to admit. 'I knew she was coming.'

'And you never said!' His eyes reproached her.

There was no way she could explain in public, and with Vicky there, gaping at him and devouring his face with her eyes, and besides, if she didn't hurry, she would be late on duty.

Kirk said, 'I presume you've already eaten?'

'Yes, we were just going.' Vonne rose hurriedly as she realised that this was just the opportunity Vicky wanted. 'I'm on duty at ten.'

There didn't appear to be anyone with Kirk, and presumably he had not yet had a meal. He said, 'I had a busy time this evening. I've only just got away.' His gaze rested on Vicky, who sat transfixed and speechless.

Vonne said, 'There's no need for you to come, Vicky,' and to Kirk she proposed boldly, 'Would you mind running Vicky home later? She's staying with me.' She slipped the key to the flat off her key-ring and gave it to her twin.

Kirk was sliding into the seat Vonne had vacated. She gave him no chance to object—not that she expected he would.

'Well, good night,' she said. 'See you later, Vicky.'

She escaped with her heart pounding and her emotions in worse turmoil than ever. Fate had taken a hand and had thrown Kirk and Vicky together very conveniently. In a way she was glad it had happened so soon. By tomorrow morning, it would all be resolved. She had no doubt now that Kirk and Vicky would be reconciled.

As she drove to the hospital she thought how ironic it was, that Fate had dealt her the same blow twice in her life. First there had been Leith whom she had fallen in love with, only to have his fiancée return and claim him. And now it was Kirk, who had captured her heart even more irrevocably, and who was now being claimed by *his* ex-fiancée. The worst part was that neither Leith nor Kirk had ever really belonged to her—both men had been in love with someone else all the time.

It was quiet when Vonne went on duty. Most of the patients were, as usual, asleep, and once the previous shift had gone, a stillness descended on the wards.

After checking through the written report from the previous shift, Vonne toured the wards, treading softly so as not to disturb those who were asleep, and using her torch where necessary to avoid switching on lights.

For some reason the distant hum of the air-conditioning sounded louder than usual. Vonne caught herself listening to it as one does to the rhythm of train wheels or the throbbing of a jet-plane's engines, and after a while she began hearing a hiccup that wasn't quite normal. It was only because of the slight malfunction that she was conscious of it at all.

'I don't like the sound of the air-conditioning,' she said to Jill as they were having a cup of coffee around two a.m. 'I hope it isn't on the blink.'

Jill listened. 'It does sound a bit odd,' she commented,

adding, 'Isn't it quiet tonight? Quieter than usual somehow. Makes you think of the calm before a storm.'

'I hope not! We're in the cyclone season now, aren't
we?'

'Yes, November to March—Tracy was on Christmas
Eve. But there've been no warnings. We'd get plenty of
notice. Don't worry. No, I meant the storm we're most
likely to get will be a dozen prems all deciding to arrive at
four a.m.'

'Heaven forbid!' Vonne exclaimed. She was in no
state to cope with crises, she thought.

Jill asked how the day with Vicky had gone, and
Vonne told her what they had done. All the time she was
wondering if Kirk and Vicky were still together, if they
had gone to his place. She tried to erase the picture from
her mind, but in the stillness and quietness of the night,
there were no distractions to ease the pain caused by her
imagination.

Presently she got up and did her rounds again, even
though it wasn't necessary. She simply had to do something active to stop her imagination working overtime.
As she quietly closed one of the ward doors, she sniffed
in puzzlement. What was that strange smell?

She met Jill back at the nurses' station and was
surprised to see alarm in her face.

'Can you smell something burning?' asked Jill,
wrinkling her nose.

'Yes—I was just trying to place what it was. You're
right, it is burning—acrid like paint or . . .' Vonne stopped, listening. 'Jill, the air-conditioning has gone off.'

Jill directed her torch beam upwards towards one of
the ceiling vents which were in shadow since they only
had a desk lamp on. In a hushed, incredulous whisper,
she said,

'Look, Vonne—smoke!' Her voice became shrill with
panic. 'There's smoke coming out of the ventilator! Oh,
my God, the hospital's on fire!'

CHAPTER TWELVE

'JILL,' said Vonne in a quiet, calm voice, with as much
authority as she could muster, 'there's no need to panic.
We don't even know there's an emergency yet. It may be
nothing to worry about.' She gripped the young nurse's
arm and tried to keep a cool head herself, although
instinctive fear was squeezing her inside.

'What do we do?' squeaked Jill, the alarm in her face
turning to real fright.

'We don't panic,' repeated Vonne, relaxing her grip
and speaking in an unnaturally steady voice that didn't
seem to belong to her at all. 'We know the fire drill, all
we have to do is follow the instructions we've learnt.
The hospital isn't going to burn down in seconds. The
first thing to do is give the alarm.' She picked up the
phone. 'You'd better start alerting the patients now, just
in case, but for heaven's sake don't alarm them too
much.'

Jill was quivering and seemed unable to move. She
stood transfixed while Vonne reported the smoke
coming through the air-conditioning ventilator. When
Jill still hadn't moved as she put the phone down, Vonne
grasped her shoulders and gave her a gentle shake.
'Move, Jill! Come on. We wake everyone up and we tell
them it's just a precaution, and we evacuate them the
moment the alarm sounds. It might only be a minor
blaze that can be put out without fuss.'

Her words seemed to reassure Jill at last. The moment
of hysteria passed and she bit her lip. 'Sorry,' she
muttered.

But their hopes that it was a minor outbreak were
quickly dashed. Even as the two nurses hurried to alert

the patients, the general fire alarm resounded through the building.

'That means everybody out,' said Vonne grimly, 'but don't use the lifts. Don't let anyone use the lifts, Jill.'

She was afraid that Jill might panic again now that the alarm was real, but the young nurse seemed to have got a grip on herself and she was now all calm efficiency.

In a matter of seconds all the patients were mustered in the corridor and she was escorting them towards the fire escape stairs. Smoke was wafting along the corridors and filling the wards. Everyone was coughing.

Then somebody screamed hysterically, 'My baby— where's my baby!' and for a moment or two it looked as though the orderly evacuation would turn into a stampede as the women tried to reach the nursery.

Vonne endeavoured to calm them, but her reassurances that the nursery would be evacuated more quickly and safely if they obeyed instructions seemed to fall on deaf ears. Until, miraculously it seemed, a strong male voice came to her rescue. Eerily through the increasing smoke, Vonne saw Kirk and beside him Vicky. Then the lights went out and there were fresh cries of alarm. Kirk used stronger tones to reassure everyone, and it worked.

Vicky called out, 'I'll help get them out, Vonne.'

And then Kirk was at her side in the beam of her torch. 'Any that can't walk out by themselves?' he asked urgently.

'No . . .' Her answer was cut short by the wail of fire engines arriving on the scene.

'Is it bad?' she asked fearfully.

'I don't know. I'll see what I can do elsewhere.'

He was going, and she couldn't help herself. She cried, 'Kirk!'

'What?'

'Take care . . .' She thrust her torch at him. 'You might need this.'

Almost roughly he caught hold of her arm. 'Thanks. Now, get out of here—quickly!'

He was gone, and she stumbled along the corridor, feeling her way in the dark, making her way by instinct to the stairs. People were pouring out of other wards, some were being carried by orderlies and medical staff, and there was pandemonium on the stairs. The smell of burning was strong now, and it was stiflingly hot. Some people were becoming affected by the smoke.

Vonne supported a half-fainting elderly woman caught up in the crush on the stairs. But finally they reached fresh air, which she inhaled in great gulps. People were standing around stunned as flames leapt through the roof of the hospital. A dozen fire trucks were fighting the blaze.

As she helped the patient she was assisting towards the ambulances which were arriving to ferry patients to other hospitals, Vonne saw Vicky briefly as she shepherded others towards them too. Vonne gave her patient into the care of an ambulance man and started back to help Vicky. As she did so a woman suddenly broke away and ran screaming towards the front entrance of the hospital.

'My baby! My baby! I've got to get my baby!' Her hysterical scream rose above the crackling of the fire and the roar of the fire hoses. Before Vonne or anyone else could stop her she had plunged back into the building. Without even stopping to think, Vonne dashed after her. As she reached the entrance, strong arms halted her.

'Where the hell do you think you're going?' It was Kirk. He looked incredulously into her face when he saw who it was. 'Vonne!'

'It's Mrs Forde,' she gasped. 'She's gone back in to save her baby!' He had evidently not seen the woman run into the building or heard her scream.

'But they're all out, and safe. I checked myself.'

'She doesn't know that!' Desperately Vonne wrenched away from him and dived through the doorway which was belching thick black smoke.

There were no flames in this part of the building, but the smoke was a worse hazard.

Vonne heard Kirk yell, 'Vonne, you little fool!' as, holding a handkerchief over her nose, she groped chokingly through the smoke and darkness, realising as she did so that she probably had no hope of finding the panic-stricken woman, who might already be asphyxiated. It was her turn to panic then because she couldn't see the way out. She turned, tried to run, and tripped and as she went down, she realised she had found a body.

'Oh, my God!' she rasped, as she collapsed over it, smoke burning her eyes and throat and searing her lungs. 'Oh, Kirk,' she whispered, 'I love you so much!'

She passed out. Then she heard him call her name. She felt herself lifted in strong arms. She heard other men's voices and then she was lying down with a mask over her face and she was breathing again, although her lungs were sore and her eyes smarted painfully.

She heard a stranger's voice say, 'She's all right. She didn't get much.'

'And the other one?' Surely that was Kirk's voice.

'Not so good. She suffered longer smoke inhalation, but she'll pull through. Lucky for her the nurse found her.'

Vonne felt a blessed sense of relief. She tried to speak, but the mask hampered her. Then she heard Kirk's voice again.

'It's all right, Vonne, you're safe. Everyone is safe, including Mrs Forde.'

A few minutes later she could breathe easily again. She sat up and saw Kirk smiling at her with relief, although he sounded angry when he snapped, 'You nearly made a good job of killing yourself this time!'

'But I had to find Mrs Forde . . .'

He smoothed her hair tenderly. 'I know. You're a plucky girl. And you did find her—and I found you.'

'I only found her by accident,' Vonne told him. 'I fell over her. The smoke—it was awful . . .' On a note of panic she suddenly demanded, 'Where's Vicky?'

'She's OK. She's gone with the ambulances to Darwin Hospital where they're taking patients, to help out.'

Vonne remembered then that she had seen her sister just before she had run back into the building. She looked around. The fire hoses were still playing on the charred hospital, but the fire seemed to be under control. It was still too dark to see clearly, but the greying sky in the east presaged the dawn.

'How bad is it?' she asked, dabbing at her still watering eyes with her rather sooty handkerchief.

'Not as bad as it looks, I gather,' Kirk told her. 'But they won't know exactly until they can get back in.'

'Did everyone get out?'

'Yes. All accounted for.'

'How did it start? In the air-conditioning?'

'Apparently. Fortunately the alarm was raised quickly and they were able to bring it under control within minutes. There'll probably be more smoke and water damage than actual fire damage.' He helped her to her feet. 'We can't do any more here now. The firemen are mopping up. I think you'd better let me take you home. You need rest and something for your eyes—they're red raw.'

Vonne was still partially in shock. 'Home? Oh—yes —I suppose so.' Then she added, 'I can go, Kirk, it's only over there. You must want to . . .' She was about to say 'go and find Vicky', but she couldn't. She felt so weary all at once, and almost slumped against him.

'Come on,' said Kirk, 'I think we could both do with a cup of tea.'

She let him propel her across the lawns towards the

nurses' home. He said, 'I don't expect anyone will be allowed back for a few days at least. Fortunately the damage was confined to one area, so most of the wards can probably be opened up as soon as they've been cleaned. It seems that the storerooms and utility rooms and the main laundry were the worst affected by the flames.'

When they reached the units, Vonne suddenly remembered she didn't have her key. 'I gave it to Vicky,' she mumbled foolishly.

Kirk decided at once. 'You'd better come home with me.' Ignoring her feeble protest, he dragged her off to the car-park and pushed her into the passenger seat. Neither of them noticed Vicky's handbag which she had left there when she ran to help in the fire, and in which Vonne could have found the key.

Vonne had never been to Kirk's house. It was ironic, she thought, that she should be visiting him at home for the first time on an occasion like this. But nothing was really strange any more. It had been a bizarre night all round.

It was light when they reached Kirk's house, but Vonne could see little of the outside. It was as effectively screened by trees and shrubs as Diana's.

He ushered her into a spacious living-room, comfortably furnished with large sofas in soft tones of beige and brown. The white walls were set off with vibrant paintings of outback scenes, and she recognised the style. They were paintings by his father.

She felt strangely awkward in his private surroundings, and to cover her nervousness went up closer to one of the paintings, looking intently at it. Kirk came up behind her and her heart began to race. He placed his hands firmly on her shoulders and turned her round to face him. There was a tender expression in the hazel eyes, and he was smiling at her in a way that made her body want to melt in his arms.

She opened her mouth to speak, but couldn't remember what she had been going to say. It didn't matter, though, because he put paid to any further conversation by kissing her, so tenderly that she felt giddy. As his hands caressed her and his fingers wandered through her hair and his kiss probed deeper and deeper, seeking her response, she was powerless not to give it as before. Pressed hard against him, she responded helplessly to the touch that swept her lovingly to a pinnacle of exquisite torment.

The wrongness of it sank in only slowly. She broke away breathlessly, and exclaimed in bewilderment and anguish, 'Kirk . . . I'm not Vicky!' and covered her face with her hands in shame and despair.

But he didn't have to pretend now, she thought, as he prised her hands away and framed her face in his own large hands. Vicky was here. His fingers stroked her temples with a tantalising touch. 'I know you're not, my darling goose!'

'But, Kirk . . .' Shock seemed to have muddled them both. 'Kirk, Vicky loves you, and last night—didn't you . . . ?'

He kissed the remainder of her confusion away. 'Vicky and I had a long talk last night,' he said. 'Come and sit down and I'll tell you about it.' He examined her eyes. 'But first some soothing eye-drops. Sit down. I won't be a minute.'

Dumbfounded, she allowed him to lead her to one of the big couches. He left her for only a moment or two, returning with eye-drops which he gently dropped into her eyes.

'Now . . .' He sat down beside her and his arm encircled her as though he was afraid she would try to escape. Vonne felt light headed, as though she was dreaming.

Kirk said slowly, 'Now listen. Vicky and I had a long talk last night, as I just said. In fact we were still sitting in the car talking when the fire broke out. She was just about to go in when the alarm sounded.'

Vonne had wondered how they both had arrived on the scene so quickly, but there hadn't been time to ask. 'But surely you were . . .'

'Reconciled?' He smiled. 'That's what you expected, didn't you? Well, so did Vicky at first. Apparently you'd led her to believe that I was still in love with her.' He frowned sternly.

'I thought you were.'

'Even after I kissed you?' He sounded outraged.

'I—I thought I was just a substitute for Vicky,' Vonne said slowly, 'and that because we were so alike you couldn't quite believe I wasn't her. I thought you wanted me to be her—and at first I didn't want to be . . .'

'Is that why you ran away from me that day at Walparoo?' Astonished realisation flashed into his eyes.

'Yes. I—I didn't want to be second-best. I didn't want to be a substitute for Vicky. You called out "Vicky!" that day when you thought I was in danger, so I knew it was still her you were thinking of.'

He was perplexed. 'Did I really call her name? But that was only a slip of the tongue, believe me, Vonne. It was you, my darling, that I feared for.' He touched her face lightly. 'Yes, I see you could have read more into that, and other things perhaps, than was there.' He paused, then said thoughtfully, 'But the last time you came to Walparoo, you seemed—well, I thought you were getting over Bart. Why did you come?' He knew the answer, but he waited for her to say it.

'Because I didn't care any more if I was second-best. I—I love you so much . . .' She buried her head against his chest and whispered, 'Oh, Kirk!'

He held her tightly against him and was silent for a moment. Then he said tenderly, 'What a precious little idiot you are! I'll forgive you, though. You thought I was imagining Vicky when I kissed you, right from the start, didn't you? Oh, Vonne, it was never that. You look alike, it's true, but there are subtle differences.'

He chuckled and his chest vibrated against her cheek. 'That night in London when I kissed you by mistake —remember? I'm sure now that something irrevocable was set in motion then, but I didn't realise it. After I came back to Australia, I kept wondering if I'd made a mistake getting engaged to Vicky, if in fact it hadn't been partly a defence against Lorin. I didn't tell anyone about the engagement, partly because I think, subconsciously I was unsure, or maybe I even had a premonition it wasn't going to work out. I never connected my doubts with you until you arrived. Then I realised what a profound effect you'd had on me. It was infuriating and confusing, I admit, because you looked like Vicky. I suppose if Vicky hadn't changed her mind and had come too, we might have married. I shudder to think of it now.

'At first I didn't understand the strange sensation of relief I felt when only you arrived and I discovered that she'd jilted me.' He laughed ruefully. 'I didn't acknowledge it at first, of course. I confess my pride was a bit injured. I was more than ready to wring her pretty little neck, at least temporarily—especially as she hadn't even had the guts to tell me herself.'

'But you went on taking it out on me,' protested Vonne. 'You punished me because you couldn't punish Vicky—subconsciously you used me as a substitute for her.' She tilted her head up to challenge him.

He denied it. 'No. I'm just a little short-tempered at times. Your imagination did the rest. If I was ever abrasive with you deliberately, it was punishment for gadding about with Bart Webb—and all those others! I was jealous! That's how I knew I was falling in love with you.

'When you told me you'd been jilted too, I was shocked. And relieved. I thought maybe Bart didn't mean as much to you as I'd imagined, that I might stand a chance. And then you declared you *were* in love with him! I was perplexed. I even thought you must be as fickle as your twin sister.'

'Oh, Kirk . . .'

'How you could kiss me as you did and then say you loved someone else was beyond me,' he said, still looking outraged.

'But I didn't love anyone else. I loved you,' Vonne said simply.

He tilted her chin and kissed her lightly. 'Before we digress into pleasanter things, the rest of the story. I told Vicky that I too had realised our engagement was a mistake and that we couldn't pick up the pieces. I told her I was in love with you. She wasn't even surprised. She even said she was pretty sure you weren't as indifferent to me as you pretended.' He looked into her eyes and asked sternly, 'Did you mean what you said a moment ago?'

'From the bottom of my heart.'

She slid her arms around him and they held each other close. A long kiss later Kirk whispered, 'Is this for real, Vonne? Are you sure?'

'So very, very sure,' she said, then soberly, 'But, Vicky, Kirk . . .' How humiliated and hurt her sister must be feeling right now!

'I think Vicky had already realised that she'd been building up another romantic notion of me after Armand let her down. She practically admitted it. I don't think you need to worry about Vicky being jealous, my love, or carrying a torch for me. She has yet to find her happiness, but I'm sure she will one day.'

'I hope so,' Vonne said fervently. 'Oh, Kirk, I hope so!'

She snuggled up against him, holding him close, almost afraid to believe that what she had dreamed of was actually true. She was no substitute now, this was absolutely for real, and she had no doubts about it. Kirk wouldn't be here holding her in his arms if it wasn't.

He bent his lips to hers and a tidal wave of happiness flooded over her. There were no more words between them for a long time.

At last he murmured huskily, 'My darling, I could stay here all day with you, and let the rest of the world go hang, but I'm afraid we can't. We must have some breakfast, and you must get some sleep, and we must find Vicky, and . . .'

Vonne touched her lips tenderly to his, cutting off his words. She wound her arms around his neck, pulling him closer still.

'Just one more kiss,' she whispered dreamily, 'to convince me I'm not dreaming.' She drew his head down closer, urging him to match his lips to hers.

Kirk needed no persuasion.

She had everything a woman could want... except love.

Locked into a loveless marriage, Danica Lindsay tried in vain to rekindle the spark of a lost romance. She turned for solace to Michael Buchanan, a gentle yet strong man, who showed her friendship.

But even as their souls became one, she knew she was honour-bound to obey the sanctity of her marriage, to stand by her husband's side while he stood trial for espionage even though her heart lay elsewhere.

WITHIN REACH
another powerful novel by Barbara Delinsky, author of Finger Prints.

Available from October 1986
Price: $2.95. W⊕RLDWIDE